CHARLESTON & OTHER STORIES

CHARLESTON & OTHER STORIES BY JOSE DONOSO, 1924-

TRANSLATED BY ANDREE CONRAD

DAVID · R · GODINE
BOSTON

First published in 1977 by David R. Godine, Publisher

306 Dartmouth Street, Boston, Massachusetts

First published in Spanish as Cuentos

by Editorial Seix Barral, S.A., Barcelona, Spain.

ISBN 0–87923–197–1

LCC 76–19449

Assistance for the translation of this volume was given by the Center for Inter-American Relations.

Printed in the United States of America

ANA MARÍA

I

'STRANGE they should leave such a little girl all alone in such a big garden,' the old man thought. He wiped the sweat from his face with a handkerchief, afterwards returning it to the pocket of his tattered jacket.

In fact, the little girl was tiny, she couldn't have been more than three years old, and she was like a molecule that floated for one instant and disappeared the next among the trunks of the chestnuts and walnuts, there in the depths of the blue shadows cast by the foliage. The old man's eyes looked for the child: she seemed to have been devoured by the vegetal disorder, by the silence invaded only by the buzzing of insects and the rush of a culvert lost in the clumps of undergrowth and brambles. The man became uneasy when he couldn't spot her. But soon his eyes found the small figure crouching in a pool of yellow flowers that counterfeited a patch of sunlight in the deepest shadows. Then the old man sighed with relief, murmuring, 'Poor little thing . . . !'

He sat underneath the willow that grew on a corner of the property, casting its shadow on the sidewalk. He went about building a small fire out of dried branches, and set a tin can on it to heat up his tea. He produced a hunk of bread, tomatoes, and an onion, and began to eat, thinking it was strange he had never seen the little girl before. He had always thought this property fenced in with barbed wire was deserted, although sometimes he thought he could see a house in the depths of the trees, a sort of temporary shack that wasn't worthy of its surroundings. He had watched the garden on more than one occasion, surprised that he never saw anyone. After a while he stopped being surprised.

Every day he went to have lunch under the willow and take a nap beside this island of green, the only wooded area in the neighborhood. And at two in the afternoon he went back to the housing project where he worked two blocks down a street which was still mostly barren and not built up.

The man stretched out face down next to the barbed wire. Protected from the brutal noontime heat, he listened to the sound of the culvert and, alert to the smallest movement of the leaves, watched the garden. In the distance, he saw the little girl, who seemed to have sprouted up spontaneously as part of the vegetation. Tiny and nearly naked, she was standing near a fat tree trunk up which a red rosebush climbed with almost animal urgency. He watched her for a long while: she would slip through the bushes, she would suddenly drift away, a particularly dense shadow would dilute her small white body. Later on, the man rinsed the can and, after stamping out what was left of the fire, he went back to work.

At the end of the day, the old man didn't leave with the group of workmen as they streamed away laughing. He lagged behind to stand in front of the garden, trying to spot the little girl. But he couldn't find her.

In the evening, he sat down for a smoke beside the doorway of the shack where he lived, at the opposite end of the city. His wife, squatting in the doorway, blew on a brazier where she would set a pot of food when the coals turned red. The old man didn't know whether to tell her or not. After thirty years and more of marriage, he never had learned what he could tell his wife without making her angry . . . even though he had long since grown indifferent to his wife's fits of temper. Then he told her he had seen a very little girl in a very big garden.

'All alone?' For an instant some furrows softened the woman's face.

'And she was blonde . . .' the man added in a low voice.

Hearing her husband's tone, the hardness closed in on the woman's face again, and she blew fiercely into the brazier, so that a tail of sparks exploded into the miserable night. Then she went inside to get the pot of food, now more than ever certain of her husband's contempt. This was, without doubt, the hour she had forever been expecting, when the man, sick of silently despising her failure as a woman, would call her 'mule.' That's what the neighborhood women called her in their pride; crushed under the burden of feeding innumerable children, they always avoided associating with her; she was so sour and silent. As the years went by, she had disappeared behind a cloud of bad temper and desolation, waiting for the moment she would have to step aside and give way to another who deserved it more. In the beginning, when they were still young, the man had pitied her a little. Afterwards, it was too hard to get through to her. And as they grew older, the distance between them broadened until an almost mute bitterness was the only tangible and positive link between them.

That night the woman grudgingly served her husband a plate of soup. He spooned it up, this time unaware it was the same soup as always, the soup that in all his years of married life he had never grown to like. Then they lay down to sleep. The woman always twitched and talked to herself while she slept, which often made it difficult for the man to doze off. But sometimes she lay tense and awake for hours on end; then she didn't move. The night the man told her he had seen a very small girl alone in a very big garden, the woman lay mute and still, as if waiting.

Every day at lunchtime, the man stretched out on the sidewalk shaded by the willow near the barbed wire, looking into the garden. Sometimes he saw the girl in the distance, nearly naked, always alone, floating around in that island of plant light. But other times he didn't see her because he fell asleep, his aged body weakened by the heat and the day's work. Since he hadn't anybody else to talk to, it happened that several times he said something about the little girl to his wife, whose spirit was shriveling more and more, until nothing but bitterness was left between them.

One day the man woke up with a start underneath the willow. He scanned the denseness of the garden without seeing anybody. But suddenly, behind the barbed wire, in the darkest shadow of a bush, he saw two huge eyes, deep and clear, staring at him from the darkness. Fear unnerved him.

They were the little girl's eyes. Her body detached itself from the green reflections of the leaves. The man, ashamed, as if there were something wrong with sleeping under somebody else's willow, stood up to leave. But before he could get away, the little girl had run to the barbed wire, exclaiming: 'Sweetheart!'

He smiled out of the astonishment lying dormant within him.

'Pwetty . . . !'

The little girl's eyes were so big and clear that they fairly glowed in the small face ringed by a blonde mop. The two of them stood there frozen, looking at each other. Then the old man asked: 'What's your name, little lady?'

She didn't understand at first and the man had to repeat his question. This time the little girl answered, smiling: 'Ana María . . .'

Unable to resist, the old man inserted a hand between strands of barbed wire to caress Ana María's hair. She grew serious, as if thinking. Then, laughing, she looked him straight in his astonished eyes and showed him a bag she had dangling from her arm.

'Puss . . . puss . . . !' she exclaimed.

'What a pretty purse you have, little lady!'

'Pwetty! You pwetty, sweetheart!' Ana María exclaimed.

And, drawing away from the barbed wire that was almost dissolved by the leaves' shadows, she waved goodbye to the old man. Then she was lost amid the garden shrubbery.

'Poor little thing!' the old man said to himself.

That night he told his wife the little girl was named Ana María. He didn't say anything else to her. But the woman's body, savagely humiliated, huddled over the fire where she was boiling the laundry. Later she told her husband they had nothing to eat that night. But this was no novelty for the old man, and he went to bed early, because when he was asleep he didn't feel hungry. The woman lay down silent and motionless beside him.

2

IN BACK of the garden, Ana María's mother and father were stretched out beside each other in the narrow, messy bed. The hint of underwater light filtering through the closed green shutters fell on their sweaty bodies and flooded the tiny bedroom. A persistent hum of flies and bumblebees kept the air pulsating, humid with the odor of exhausted bodies and cigarettes and dirty sheets.

The man moved slightly. He passed a hand over his chest and stomach to dry the sweat, and as he wiped his palm on the dirty pillow he made a disgusted face without opening his eyes. Then he opened them slowly, and rolled over on his side to look at his wife's body. It was beautiful, beautiful and white. Maybe too big and fleshy, but beautiful, and where it touched the sheet the contour of her body was underlined by a fold of heavy, abundant flesh. The man knew she was only half asleep. On her pale skin, where her neck met her body, one of his own hairs was stuck, black, potent, curly. He slowly pulled it away, leaving on her skin a light reddish furrow which slowly faded. Then, with light flicks, he killed several tiny green insects that had flown in from the fastnesses of the fertile, luxuriant garden, and had settled on his wife's skin. An almost invisible specimen had alighted on her armpit, which was exposed because she slept with her arms crossed behind her head. He squashed it with deliberate pressure. The woman smiled. He caressed the hair in her armpit, and the underside of her arm, which was even whiter than the rest of her body. The woman rolled toward her husband and they lay embraced.

Then they dozed off again. Finally, opening his eyes wide, the man exclaimed: 'It's two in the afternoon! I'm hungry!'

The woman stretched, murmuring through a yawn: 'I don't think we have anything to eat . . .'

The two of them yawned in unison.

'I saw some eggs . . .'

'But I gave the kid eggs this morning . . .'

'Oh well, who cares,' said the man, rolling over and falling asleep with one heavy leg on his wife's thigh.

She freed herself from his weight and sat up vaguely, leaving a perspiration stain on the sheet. She leaned over her husband's wide, hard back and her fingers played on his shoulder muscles. But no. After some thought, she made an effort. She picked up a comb lying on the floor near the bed, next to the clam shell full of half-smoked cigarette butts, and in one practiced movement she gathered her damp hair on the back of her neck. Then she pushed her feet into her dirty white high-heeled shoes, and, naked, headed for the kitchen.

In fact, there was nothing but eggs in the icebox. Seeing the dirty dishes from breakfast that morning and from dinner the night before, she shrugged and took out clean plates so she wouldn't have to wash anything. As she cooked she tuned the radio in to a program of loud dance music. She kept time with the heel of her shoe, and her naked body vibrated as she scrambled the eggs.

'You woke me up with your damn music!' the man shouted from the bedroom.

'Too bad! You've slept enough for one day!'

The man got up. He began to do exercises in front of a long mirror. Between flexings, he asked: 'Hey. Where do you suppose the kid is?'

'Around . . .' the woman answered. 'It's Sunday, so she knows she isn't supposed to bother us . . .'

'She's too little to know it's Sunday!'

'But she knows she mustn't bother us when you're here.'

The woman put down two plates for her husband and her daughter. She served herself in a cup because she couldn't find another clean plate and she couldn't bring herself to wash one. She put on a robe, her husband some undershorts, and after she shouted from the doorway for Ana María to come in, the three of them sat down at the small table in the living room, where they generally ate.

When Ana María saw the eggs, she said: 'Don't want any.'

But they didn't listen to her, because they were laughing at some cartoons in a magazine. Later the woman saw that Ana María hadn't eaten and was staring at her with those enormous, clear, transparent eyes. She felt uncomfortable and snapped: 'Eat!'

Ana María looked at the eggs and said again: 'Don't want any.'

'Well, take some bread then, and get out.'

Ana María left.

'Did she eat this morning?' the man asked.

'Yes, I think so. I was a little fuzzy, so I didn't notice . . .'

'Fuzzy? Why?'

'You ask why after last night? Dummy!'

They laughed.

'Hurry up and wash the dishes.'

'Not likely. I suppose you think I married you to wait on you and the kid . . .'

Leaving everything in the same turmoil as before, they went back to the bedroom. After a few moments of ambiguous games and dozing, the man suggested: 'Hey. Want to go to the movies tonight?'

'Okay, but we'll have to make sure the kid is asleep first, and locked in.'

'Okay . . . that's what we always do.'

'Yes. But she's being so strange, I don't know what could be the matter with her. Haven't you noticed? Sometimes I think she's . . . I don't know . . . she almost scares me. You know the other day when we got back from the movies she was awake, she was only pretending to be asleep, and it was nearly one in the morning . . .'

'So? What's so odd about that?'

'I don't know, she's just awfully little.'

'Don't be silly. Anyway, what difference does it make? She's got all day to sleep if she feels like it.'

'She's always been a little strange. The way she talks is a little babyish for her age. And you know the only thing she likes to play with is that bag where I keep her shoes. . . . God knows what she sees in it. . . . Puss, she calls it.'

'Mmm . . . she's a strange kid, all right . . .'

'And a bit of a pain, too, when she stares at me with those animal eyes of hers. Only yesterday I dozed off on that canvas chair in the garden . . . You know this heat makes me so sleepy . . . ?'

'Only sleepy?'

Laughing, the woman patted the moist fur on her husband's chest.

'. . . Anyway, I fell asleep. Suddenly I woke up. The first thing I saw, a ways off under that linden tree, was the kid, or rather the kid's eyes, watching me like a moron from the shadows. When she realized I was awake, she ran away.'

'God, what a ninny you are. What's wrong with that?'

'I don't know, but it sure is odd. And the other day. You know she hovered around me all morning long waiting for me to pick her up or something, but didn't say anything or come close to me. But I didn't feel much like doing anything, I felt a little tired, you know . . .'

'When don't you, you lazy slut!'

'. . . So anyway, I picked her up. Then she began to hug me and giggle and make such a fuss over me in such a sticky way that I felt . . . I don't know, kind of scared or maybe disgusted. But sometimes she's awfully cute, you know. And she was saying "Sweetheart" and "Pwetty" to me, you know, the first words she learned, who knows where, because you sure never say them to me . . .'

'Never? What?'

'No. Never.'

'But I say nicer things to you.'

'Yes, but not that. Anyway, she was all over me with kisses and I was just petrified, when guess what she did?'

'What?'

'She bit my ear.'

The man laughed. 'She bit your ear? How could that little devil know you like it?'

'Don't be an ass, not like that. Don't laugh. She didn't just nibble at it, she bit it damn hard, as if she wanted to bite it right off with those tiny sharp teeth she has. It hurt so much I screamed and dropped her. And she bolted away, as if she knew she'd done something wrong. That was in the morning. She didn't come in for lunch, or all day long. And you know how I hate to go out in the garden among those trees, so I didn't go looking for her. But when she sneaked in that night, I punished her . . .'

'What did you do to her?'

'How should I know? Am I supposed to remember everything?'

The man laughed again, this time at another cartoon in the illustrated magazine which he had been leafing through as they talked. He felt the moist contours of his wife's body next to his own. They had a smoke, and one of them went to get the radio so they could listen to music. The green light coming through the shutters from the garden began to wane.

3

THE OLD man went to the willow tree every day to have lunch. He didn't have to scour the garden anymore because the child was always waiting for him beside the barbed wire. Somehow she seemed to know what time it was, and if the man was late she gave him a scolding look. But soon she would smile at him, murmuring: 'Sweetheart. Pwetty.'

The old man gathered his strength and lifted Ana María over the fence to sit her down beside him. He let her light the fire to heat up the tea. Then he ate his bread, occasionally a piece of meat, onions, and tomatoes, sharing his meal with her, because she always seemed hungry.

A worker from his construction site once surprised him in his tête-à-tête with Ana María. After that, none of the workers would let him alone.

'Hey, you smitten old duffer! How's your girlfriend?'

He listened to their laughter patiently. As he pushed around his wheelbarrow, his ancient, trembling legs barely kept him from falling down the ramp. His eyes, smudged with dirt and sweat, could hardly see the young workers who jeered at him from the girders: 'Hey, you old devil! Watch out, or they'll throw you in prison!'

And thinking about what Ana María had said to him at lunchtime, he blushed under the filth on his face.

The child had sat down next to him in the shade, quickly opening her ever-present bag to show him a pair of shoes.

'Soos! Pwetty foot?'

Inside the bag, there was also a tattered but shiny ribbon. With numb hands the old man tied it around the girl's blonde hair and she proudly felt the knot of the light blue ribbon. The child showed him some other things, too: a die, a box of Band-Aids, another of matches, the severed head of a doll. That was the last thing she took out of the bag, as if she didn't want her friend to see it, as if she herself didn't want to look at it. It was a blonde head, fat-cheeked, a sensual, self-satisfied face.

'And what's this, little lady?'

Ana María's eyes suddenly filled with tears, which hung there without falling, magnifying her eyes.

'Bad . . .' the little girl murmured.

'Why bad?'

Then she vehemently shook the broken toy, crying out: 'Bad, bad, bad!' And she threw it into the garden thickets. Just then her eyes welled over and she stood still, looking at the old man, her cheeks soaked and her eyelashes wet.

The old man took Ana María in his arms, cuddling her head on his shoulder, until he soothed the quiet sobbing. He wiped away her tears with his own handkerchief. Then the child caressed his furrowed, unshaven face with her hand and said: 'Pwetty . . . pwetty, sweetheart.'

After that, the old man went back to work, happy.

In the evenings, having a smoke in the doorway of his shack, he would watch the darkness fall on the ramshackle roofs of the neighborhood. There he thought about the child, such a little girl alone in such a big garden. Without making plans, without dwelling on incidents, he opened himself up completely so that the presence of Ana María could fill him. And his wife ferociously watched him almost without looking at him, certain that the time was approaching when she would leave, would give way to another.

Time passed and the building project where the old man worked was completed. They dismissed the workers, most of whom found other jobs right away, but nobody wanted to give work to anybody as feeble as the old man. He understood the situation but didn't worry about it. What bothered him was the thought of Ana María waiting for him beside the barbed-wire fence at the other end of the city, to talk to him for a while, to have some bread and onions with him.

The old man's wife was a laundress and she supported both of them. The old man was sure she would never throw his idleness in his face, despite his silence, which had become a solid wall between them. The woman said nothing because she had no right to demand anything. She just watched him sitting in the doorway morning, noon, and night, thinking. With his hands resting slack on each knee, his face smiling a little, he seemed to be counting the seconds contained in each hour. The old man's lips moved almost imperceptibly. 'Poor little thing!' the old woman read on them, and in those words meant for another, she found her own condemnation.

Two or three times, the old man went to see the little girl. He stole a piece of bread from his wife, and, muttering between his teeth that he was going out to look for work, he was off early in the morning. The woman knew he was lying.

The old man trudged along, resting once in a while under a tree in a park, picking up a discarded newspaper to read while he rested. And when he was ready, he trudged onward, and at last he had crossed the entire city and was at the garden where Ana María waited for him, at the same hour as their former lunches under the willow tree.

The first thing the old man saw was always her deep blue eyes, bright and furtive among the branches. Seeing him approach, the little girl happily ran forward to have her friend lift her over the fence. Then, as they ate and talked under the willow tree, it was as if nothing in the world could disturb them.

The woman could not tolerate the situation any longer. The little that was left of her never very generous world, which had dwindled over the years, finally collapsed. She spent her days working hard, furiously, to kill everything inside her that dared to feel. But before giving in completely to the inevitable, some hidden embers of energy pushed her to a decision.

One day she bought a bag of candy and, taking the bus, went to the garden near the building project. She installed herself underneath the willow tree. It really was big and green, that garden, a lushness of trees and freshness and deep shade. Near her, under the willow, dark spots attested to the fires over which her husband had warmed his tea. She sat down to wait.

Soon she saw the little girl in the distance, wading in the culvert, her white body wounded by the reflections from the water. At the sight of her, the woman's heart knotted up in astonishment, silence, hatred. She stood next to the barbed wire so that Ana María would see her and come over.

Ana María didn't look at her. She climbed out of the culvert, and little by little, the woman didn't know how, she wove through the bushes and brambles, coming closer to the willow. But she kept her distance.

Then the woman saw the deep blue eyes staring hard at her from the shade, trapping her in their hostile clarity. With a last effort, the woman dragged out a smile from somewhere inside herself. But the little girl stood motionless behind the bushes, watching.

The woman faltered. The whole thing was futile. Everything was always futile. As a last resort, she pulled out the candy, saying: 'Would you like a piece of candy, little girl?'

The child shook her head no. The woman persisted: 'They're very sweet . . .'

'Don't want any,' Ana María answered.

Finally, the whole mask of desolation and failure fell over the woman's face. She turned to leave. Just then the little girl took a few steps forward.

'Bad! Bad! Bad!' she cried, staring straight at her. And the woman fled, defeated.

When she arrived home she told the old man a family she did laundry for had offered her a live-in job, so she wouldn't ever lack for food or a roof over her head. Also, a neighbor wanted to rent the shack they lived in. She was leaving the next day. They sat in silence. After a while, the old man seemed to hear the woman asking him from a corner of the room: 'What about you, what are you going to do?'

'I don't know,' he answered out loud.

And the woman looked at him, surprised.

It had been a month since he had been to see the little girl. He was so old that it seemed he grew tireder with every hour. Walking to the opposite side of the city seemed almost beyond his strength.

But in the morning, when his wife would no longer exist, he would go say goodbye to the little girl. After that, nothing mattered. Maybe the best thing would be to go to some deserted place, to a hillside, say, and wait for nightfall and then die. He was certain that merely by curling up on the ground and wishing for it, death would come.

The next day he took the last piece of bread and walked more slowly than ever to Ana María's garden. It was Sunday. The people taking refuge under the shade of trees in parks didn't look at him; it seemed he no longer existed.

As if he had never gone away, the little girl was waiting for him next to the barbed-wire fence. And just as he had been the first time, he was astonished at the sight of such a little girl alone in such a big garden.

'Poor little thing!' he said to himself, coming closer.

'Sweetheart!' the little girl murmured at the sight of him.

He lifted her over the fence, and Ana María kissed and hugged him, laughing.

'My pretty lady!' the old man exclaimed over and over, stroking her with his dark hands. 'Where's your little purse?'

Ana María's face clouded over. She raised her shoulders and said: 'No . . . nothing . . .'

They sat together for a long time in the shade of the willow, until finally the old man thought it was time for him to go. He put her down on the other side of the fence. And, caressing her blonde head through the wire, he said: 'Goodbye, little lady . . .'

She looked at him startled, as if she understood.

'No, no, sweetheart, no,' she said, her eyes magnified by tears.

'Goodbye,' he repeated.

Ana María held onto the old man's hand tightly. But suddenly, as if she had a plan, she smiled. Her tears dried and she said: 'Wait, wait. Puss . . .'

The old man watched his little friend disappear into the vegetation, thinking it would be the last time he'd see the tiny girl running alone through the treetrunks and bushes of the big garden.

Ana María opened the door and went into the living room, muttering 'Puss . . . puss . . .' as she searched the kitchen, the bedroom, the closet. But she couldn't find it.

She hesitated a second before going into her parents' room. But then she pushed the door open. In the green light populated with buzzes, the couple parted abruptly, and ashamed and furious on seeing the child, they half-covered themselves with the sheet. The woman glared at the child in the doorway.

'Stupid kid!' she screamed, sitting up.

Her hair was a mess. She covered herself with a corner of the sheet.

'Don't you know you're not supposed to bother us?' the man shouted.

'Puss!' said Ana María, looking around the room, which was heavy with the scent of her parents' intimacy.

'I told you I don't want you playing with that bag. You'll lose it. Now get out of here!'

'Give her the goddamn bag so she'll get out of here,' the man mumbled, drawing the sheet farther up.

'There it is, on the chair. Now get out.'

The child grabbed the bag and ran out without looking at her parents, who sank back into the bed, relieved but uncomfortable. Ana María ran through the garden, jumped, flew, over the culvert exposing herself to discs of light that floated down through the branches. The old man waited for her beside the barbed wire. The little girl said to him: 'Hup, hup!'

The old man lifted her over to his side. He trembled a little because he was very old and he knew what was going to happen, and he didn't know so many other things. Ana María sat on the ground and took her shoes from the bag.

'Soos. Put on soos,' she pleaded with the old man.

The old man kneeled to put her shoes on with his numb fingers. Then the two of them stood up under the willow, the stooped and dark old man beside the little girl with the bag hanging on her arm. He looked at her expectantly. Then Ana María smiled as she had in better times, from the depths of her phosphorescent blue eyes.

'Sweetheart,' she said.

And taking the old man by the hand, she led him out of the willow's shade and into the brutal heat of the summer afternoon. She led him forward, towing him along, and said to him: 'Wet's go, wet's go . . .'

The old man followed her.

SUMMERTIME

I

'SO WHAT did *she* say?' asked the older of the two nannies while she knitted, comfortably settled on a blanket where the beach was dry. The younger nanny didn't answer at once. She was scanning the water's edge for Raulito, who didn't seem to be with his cousins. After a moment she spotted him, squatting beside a hole he was digging in the sand. Then she answered, mimicking her employer:

'"How dare that shameless tart rent a house down here! As if everybody didn't know what kind of a trollop she is!" She was just fit to be tied, Juanita. Don Raul didn't dare look at her. How she carried on! I don't know why she doesn't swallow her jealousy and let it go at that. Naturally the girl is pretty. A blonde. She looks like an actress.'

Juana moved her blanket closer to her young companion, who was wearing earrings that tinkled, and said: 'I've seen the girl. She bleaches it. But do you really think *she*'s right, Carmen?'

'Maybe . . . maybe not.' Carmen weighed the question. 'Could be one of those rich ladies' fantasies. They got nothing to do but spend the whole day imagining things. Now, it's true before the girl came two nights ago, Don Raul was always *so* busy in Santiago. Let's see how he behaves now.'

Juana waited for Carmen to tell all. After a pause, she said invitingly: 'Wonder how it all started . . .'

'Well, this I got from other people, you know. They say it happened over Christmas, at a dance. So the thing's brand new. You remember when I told you she had this long dress made which luckily makes her look thinner? Well, that's what it was for. They say Don Raul got a little tight and danced all night long with the hussy. *She* came home early, all by herself, and he sneaked in at eight in the morning.'

'For God's sake, some men are really the limit,' Juana sighed. 'And *she*'s such a good person too. Such a homebody, so religious and everything.'

'But you know, Juanita, I wouldn't know who to blame,' Carmen said. She had a beauty mark next to her lip and her long hair half-covered her earrings. A movie magazine rested on her lap. 'I can understand him. She doesn't take care of herself at all. I don't know why, when you consider the time and money she's got. Think how we have to make do with the one or two rags we can afford. She frets around the house all the time, sticking her nose in everybody's chores, for no good reason. And don't think it's because she's one of those women who worries about her child twenty-four hours a day. Not at all. Sometimes she feels like paying attention to him, sometimes she doesn't. She doesn't like to go out and spends all her time at home while he's always at the Club. So what do you think he's likely to do, eh? Find himself a honey, of course!'

Stretching out on the blanket, Carmen opened the magazine. Juanita looked at her thoughtfully. She didn't know what to make of these young girls without principles, employed one month here, one month there, only interested in smoking cigarettes on the sly and going to the movies. She would bet that Carmen's beauty mark was painted on.

The children's silhouettes began to darken against the sky and sea, which would soon be turning red. Scattered across the sand, clusters of nannies chattered and knitted. But they never lost sight of the children, who ran through the water or made castles in the wet sand. Behind them, the houses of the quiet family beach resort were half hidden among the pine trees or stood out from banks of lobelias and bougainvillea climbing up the hill. At the other end of the long stretch of beach, some kilometers away, the cliffs of the large, noisy, vulgar resort town were visible, crowned by its hotels and shoddy lookout towers.

'Going to spend Sunday in Santa Cruz?' Juana asked her companion.

Carmen raised her head, and looking at the distant town, said: 'There's nobody to go with.'

Before turning back to her reading, Carmen's eye came to rest on a young nanny coming toward them with a boy in tow.

'Look, Juanita, look. Speak of the devil. That's the blonde's child. The nanny's a friend of mine.'

She waved to her friend, standing up to greet her. Juana watched them embrace. 'Two of a kind,' she said to herself, since the newcomer was younger than Carmen and even flashier. The boy with her was tall and dark, very strong for his age; he looked about nine. While his nanny talked to Carmen, he made a whistling noise in the air with a freshly peeled branch that was still shiny and wet. Then he sat down in the sand to take off his sandals. Carmen introduced the newcomer to Juana, and in a few minutes the three of them were chattering away.

'I expect you asked for Sundays off, Rosa,' Carmen said.

'Naturally, dear, what do you take me for. That was the first thing I said to her when I found out we were going to be near Santa Cruz.'

'That's swell, then. I was just telling Juanita I didn't have anybody to go into town with. Let's be sure and go this Sunday.'

The child was sitting on the sand, a few steps away. His body was very erect, and he kept his eyes fixed on the horizon. Filling his sandals, he would hold them up and let the dry sand flow through their many holes.

'Jaime, run along and get your feet wet before it turns cold. It's getting late,' said Rosa.

'I don't want to.'

'Oh, what a pain you are!'

'It's just that he doesn't know anybody and doesn't want to play all by himself,' Juana murmured, smiling at the boy.

'I'll call Raulito to play with him,' Carmen offered. As she stood up to shout for him, she gave Juana a look of complicity.

'Come play with this little boy, Raul,' she said to the boy. Raul had great blue, trusting eyes. His legs were wet and he held a bucket. 'Lend him your shovel.'

The two boys sat down without even saying hello. The glare of the sun, reflected off the ocean, made the two boys squint, so that anyone seeing them might have thought they were angry.

'You want to play with my shovel?' Raul asked.

'No.'

'Here, take my pail and make a mound,' Raul tried again.

'I don't want to.'

Jaime stood up and made the branch whistle in the air.

'What're you doing that for?'

'That's what I do in the country,' was Jaime's answer. Then he explained. 'To cut down the blackberry shoots.'

'What do you want to do that for?'

'Just because. Blackberry shoots are bad.'

'Who says?'

'Nobody. I know what's bad.'

Raul looked fragile and gentle, very childish, beside the solid physique of the new boy. He wanted to go back to the seaside, to the castle he was building with his cousins Pia and Antonio.

'Do you know about the palace in the dunes?'

Jaime shook his head.

'It's down the beach that way,' the boy explained, thrusting his lower lip in the direction of Santa Cruz. 'I made one just like it out of sand. Of course Pia helped me, but not much. She only made the garden. You want to see it?'

'No.'

There was something of the hawk about Jaime's profile, as if he saw everything from great heights, taking in vast distances. The face of the man he would be was already present in his boyish features and in the fixed darkness of his serious, sunken eyes.

'I don't want to,' he said again.

'Go on, silly,' said Rosa, who had heard part of the conversation. But Raul was already gone. He was skipping and running along the edge of the sea, with the other children. Jaime sat down in the sand and took a slingshot out of his pocket. Gazing at it, he drew the sling several times. Then he put it away and turned back to his game with the sandals and dry sand. From time to time he looked at the edge of the water.

'Is there a real palace around here?' Rosa asked.

'It's no palace,' Juana answered. 'That's just the kids' nonsense. It's a ruined house just down the beach a ways.'

'Near Santa Cruz?'

'On the way, beside the beach. It's right near here. Tomorrow afternoon we could take the children,' Carmen suggested.

'Sure,' said Juana, who was enchanted with Rosa.

When the sun disappeared, the town receded into a liquid twilight, and the nannies called the children in. The breeze had come up and it was time to leave. As they gathered their belongings, Pia wanted to strike up a conversation with Jaime, but he wouldn't pay attention to her. The children put on their shoes sitting on the steps that led from the sand up to the road. Jaime moved over beside Raul and showed him the slingshot.

'What's that?' Raul asked, poking it.

'A slingshot,' Jaime answered.

'What's it for?'

'Tomorrow I'll tell you.'

'Good.'

As they were saying goodbye, Jaime whispered in Raul's ear: 'Do you know how to sing?'

'No.'

'I do. I'm going to teach you.'

'Okay.'

'But on one condition,' Jaime added, while the nannies finished saying goodbye.

'What's that?'

'That you always mind me, and don't play with anybody but me.'

All suspicion vanished in Raul. He never wanted to be separated from his friend.

That night, when Carmen was sprucing him up before sending him down to his parents, Raul asked her what a slingshot was.

'A stick with elastic,' was the nanny's explanation.

'But what's it for?'

'Bad little boys use them to kill birds.'

Afterwards, as he was drying his hands, Raul asked her more questions: 'Do you know how to sing, nanny?'

Carmen said yes, but not very well.

'And do only bad little boys sing?'

'What a nuisance you are, silly! Go down to your mother and ask her, Mr. Questions,' Carmen exclaimed, kissing him. They were very good friends.

Raul's mother had a headache. His father hadn't come home yet. They ate alone, without waiting for him.

That night, Raul couldn't go to sleep. He was thinking about the slingshot. As he counted eleven strokes from the church clock, he saw his mother softly opening the door of his room, putting out her cigarette before she came in. Hearing her move in the darkness around his bed, Raul murmured: 'Mama . . .'

'Shhh . . . Go to sleep, it's late.'

'Papa isn't home yet.'

She didn't answer. Tucking him in, she kissed him good night. Raul saw her rather stout silhouette in the light of the door.

The next day, on the way to the palace, Jaime and Raul lagged behind. The others, next to the white sea, under a great open sky, skipped in the water, while the seagulls wheeled high over prey visible only to their eyes. Barefoot, the children squashed the slime next to the foamy lace the tide left behind.

'My nanny says slingshots are bad,' Raul said.

'Baloney. You have to kill sparrows.'

'Why?'

'I know what's bad.'

'So how do you do it?'

'If you promise to mind everything I say, I'll show you.'

'Okay.'

They walked alongside the edge of the water. With a stroke of his branch, the taller boy released a tuft of foam. His black eyes, like two heavy stones, fell on all things, on the sea, on Raul, on bits of seashells and pebbles, absorbing everything. His fists were clenched so tight that his knuckles shone.

'I know two songs,' he explained. 'When I sing the first one, you have to laugh. Okay?'

'Okay.'

Jaime grabbed the little boy's arm hard and began to sing in a low voice. The melody his voice carried was monotonous, with hardly any high or low notes. At first, Raul tried to free his arm, but then, drawing close to Jaime, he listened. A smile brushed the edges of his light blue eyes, while the melodic line, light and short, repeated itself over and over. Jaime stared at him with the two black stones of his eyes, trapping him. Unable to control himself, Raul burst out laughing. He laughed and laughed and laughed. Jaime, who had taken his serious eyes off his friend, stared at the horizon, repeating the singsong tune. Raul kept on laughing after Jaime stopped.

'Okay,' he said. 'Now show me the slingshot.'

'No,' said Jaime. 'We're not through yet. You have to cry.'

'Okay.'

Raul moved closer to his friend, noticing that they were coming to the palace. The new melody was a slow tralala, more tense than sad. Raul's eyes filled with tears, and his sunburnt hand rose as if to dam them up. As the tralala went on repeating, getting slower and slower, the boy's tears turned into sobs.

'Okay,' said Jaime, 'that's enough.'

But his friend's sobbing went on.

'Stop crying, silly. Look, there's your nanny watching you. She's going to give you hell if she catches you crying. Come on, here's the slingshot.'

Raul's sobbing subsided. He dried his tears and pointed the house out to Jaime.

'Look, that's the palace.'

It sat on top of a small dune. Perhaps at the beginning of the century it had been a great wooden mansion, with a fine balcony and two towers facing the sea. But there wasn't much left of the house. The birds had been nesting for years among its leaden beams, flitting through what had been dining room, parlor, and bedroom. It was only a skeleton. More than thirty years had passed since anybody had lived in it, since the wind had whistled through those rooms where once voices had sounded; since the dunes had drifted over the specter of its gardens; since the winter storms had lifted off its roof; since the need of the indigent to keep themselves warm had stripped it of doors, walls, windows; and above all, since the ficklenesses of taste and fashion had transformed it into an object of ridicule. But absurd, poor, and useless as it was, it had been rescued by the compassion of those children who in the nearby resort lived in clean, neat houses; they dressed it up in the colors of legend. In the windows of the towers, at both ends of the façade, some fragments of stained glass remained where once had glowed ribbons, slave women, lotuses. In the afternoon, the wonder-time of the palace, the sun fragmented itself on those shabby bits of glass. Then, fleetingly, the two towers burned with glory, breaking up the light in thousands of reflections and drowning the melancholy, washed-out bones that were left of the house.

'Let's have a treasure hunt!'

'Let's do!' cried Pia, dropping down beside Jaime.

'How do you play it?' he asked.

'You want to play too?' Pia said slyly. She hadn't forgotten his lack of interest in her the day before. 'Oh, I thought you were a grown-up.'

'He and I are the same age,' Raul defended his friend.

'You have to look for bits of colored glass in the sand,' Pia explained, 'the kind that fall down from the palace. The green ones are worth the most because they're emeralds. You keep them in your pail.'

'I don't have a pail.'

Raul suggested the two of them work together.

'No, with me, with me, come with me,' Antonio shrieked. Antonio was Pia's younger brother, with a freckled nose and bony knees and skinny legs.

'Shut up,' Raul said. 'Jaime's coming with me.'

'No,' said Jaime, 'I'm going with the little one.'

Raul pursed his lips in a grimace of displeasure. Jaime began to sing softly. His cold eyes were fixed on the sea, and at the same time on Raul. As the song grew louder, Raul's eyes began to fill with tears. But before the others could notice it, the boy escaped in search of treasure. The rest of them scattered after him.

In a while the hunt was over and the children came out

from among the beams. Quietly, they squatted to hold their transparent treasures up to the sun. They compared shapes, sizes, colors. In one Jaime found, there was half of the face and the eye of a woman. Others were pure color. As it turned out, Jaime found more bits of glass than the others, which seemed natural. After showing the others how to make figures in the sand with them, he divided up his treasure, saying he didn't want it. Later, the four children sat down in silence, lined up in front of the ocean. A streetlight, a bottle, a boat, a house: the waning sun changed shape as it fell below the horizon.

It came time to leave. Juana rubbed Pia's sunburnt face with special unguents. Pia submitted, proud of her privilege. Jaime and Raul walked back together, separated from the others. Raul asked his friend to sing, and he did, making the little boy laugh or cry, depending on the tune. Afterwards he showed him how to use the slingshot.

2

TIME WENT by and it was the middle of summer. Jaime and Raul met at the beach every afternoon. But the mornings were different. Then, the children went down to the beach all spruced up with their parents, installing themselves in front of the family cabaña: it was the hour to do their duty. Being on display near their parents, they could hardly play with each other. One morning Raul's mother saw him with Jaime. She strictly forbade him ever to speak to Jaime again. This didn't matter much to Raul, since she never came down to the beach in the afternoon, and those were the best hours. He and Jaime would go off alone together looking for conch shells and pebbles. As the afternoon air turned restless and the sun began to burnish the pine-covered hillsides, both boys sat down on the sand and Raul said he wanted to laugh.

Jaime sang and the boy howled with laughter. After talking of many things and playing with the slingshot, Raul said he wanted to cry. Then Jaime would intone the other melody and his friend sobbed disconsolately.

One afternoon, going down to the beach, Raul asked his nanny: 'Why don't they want me to be friends with Jaime?'

'How do you know that?'

'Because my mother was fighting with my father. My father knows Jaime, but my mother doesn't want me to.'

'I don't think . . .'

'Why don't they want me to be friends with him?'

'Because he plays with slingshots, just like a poor boy.'

'That's a lie,' Raul answered, suddenly indignant. 'It isn't because of that. It's because he sings to me. You *told* on me. I don't love you anymore.'

He ran down the slope to join his cousin Pia.

Installed on the beach, Jaime and Raul remained near the nannies. Jaime had brought sweets, and insisted on sharing them with Juana and Carmen.

'It's most provoking, Rosa,' Carmen exclaimed. 'Imagine, *she* got it into her head to take a trip to the country this Sunday. That means I can't go to Santa Cruz. And we told the boys we'd meet them. They invited us to the movies and everything. What's worse, they're leaving Monday.'

'Well, isn't that a bummer,' Rosa said, piqued. 'I don't dare go alone and I don't know their address in Santa Cruz.'

'Or in Santiago either,' her friend added.

'Careful with those boys, now,' Juana admonished them.

The next day there was no beach for Raul. Nor the day after, nor the following day. For some reason he didn't grasp, every day he was sent hiking in the hills with his cousins.

One night after dinner, Carmen leaned over Raul to give him a kiss after tucking him in. He bit her ear and made her cry.

'Meany,' he said. 'You told on me.'

Carmen swore she hadn't. In tears, she assured him she was innocent. Finally she made peace with him. She kissed Raul's forehead and turned out the light on the night table. When the girl stood up in the darkness to leave, the little boy clung to her hand.

'Stay . . .' he murmured.

Outside, the night was clear. A slender branch crossed the open window and in the corners of the room the shadows played gently, crouching beside the child-sized furniture. The sea gathered everything inside the knot of its insistent sound. Raul refused to let go of Carmen's hand: he caressed her bare arm, and then placed her hand over his heart, which was palpitating under his striped pajamas. He kept her there.

'You want to go to Santa Cruz this Sunday, don't you? To go to the movies with the boys?'

Carmen was startled. She wasn't at all anxious to have *her,* with all her fine morality and churchgoing, hear about her Sunday outings. She asked Raul: 'How do you know that?'

'I heard what you were saying.'

Raul guided the girl's hand in the darkness to caress his warm neck, his ears, his salty hair. In the transparent air, the curtains kept up a light, sweet, swaying motion. The boy said: 'If you want, I'll get sick Sunday and that way there won't be any trip and you can go to the movies with the boys.'

Carmen didn't answer right away. She could feel the blue of Raul's eyes fixed on her in the darkness. She gently caressed his neck, while he stroked her bare arm. He was the dearest boy in the world. But it wasn't hard to figure out that he wanted something. She asked him. Squeezing Carmen's arm until it hurt her, he said: 'I want you to take me to the beach Monday afternoon.'

There was a silence. In the depths of it, the breakers went on thudding quietly, very close. Carmen agreed. From the floor below, the sound of voices floated up. Raul's mother had guests that night.

'I've got to go pass drinks.'

'Good night,' Raul murmured.

'Good night,' she answered.

When she leaned over in the darkness to kiss him, Raul threw his arms around her neck and felt the warm shape of her lips next to his own.

'Cute thing,' Carmen whispered when the boy's arms released her. She left the room, and he fell asleep instantly.

On Saturday, Raul showed his mother a huge bloody gash on his foot. In consternation, she said he had better stay home the next day. The outing was postponed. That night, Carmen, shocked at what the boy had done to himself, went up to his room to talk to him. She found him fast asleep, with a smile in the corners of his eyes.

Sunday, Raul's mother let him sleep late, and kept him quiet all day long. His father had suddenly returned to Santiago, and she, disheveled and in a vile temper, spent the afternoon knitting at Raul's side.

The wound in his foot was almost healed the next day. Raul said that although it didn't hurt, he would rather go down to the beach that morning, and hike in the woods to collect pine cones in the afternoon.

That afternoon, silent and somewhat annoyed, Carmen took Raul to the beach. On the way he asked: 'How was your Sunday, nanny?'

Carmen frowned and didn't answer. On the beach they had to search for Jaime, because he wasn't at the usual place. Rosa greeted her friend coldly. The nannies told the boys not to wander too far, since the afternoon was chilly and they should go home early. The two boys began to shoot pebbles with the slingshot. Raul had learned how, but his aim wasn't very good yet. They didn't talk much.

'Sing to me,' said Raul.

Jaime began to intone his song. His voice rose and fell monotonously, on and on; his hard profile remained fixed on the horizon. A cold wind was blowing, and the town, opaque, hid the rain. There was hardly a soul on the beach. Raul, his hands buried in the sand, which was dry but hard from the cold, began to cry. Jaime's song became more and more melancholy every moment, and Raul's crying turned into sobs. He sobbed as never before. Carmen, who was sunk in thought and only half concentrating on her magazine, saw him and ran over immediately.

'What's the matter?' she asked. 'Does your foot hurt?'

Jaime's song went on. He closed his eyes, and his face took on a hermetic expression. He didn't see, he didn't feel. Raul's sobs became whoops, strong and urgent as they had never been before. Indignant, Carmen shouted at Jaime: 'You're making Raulito cry, you nasty little kid,' and she took hold of him to slap him. Seeing Carmen about to spank her Jaime, Rosa ran over and yanked him away. 'What gives you the right to hit the little boy?'

'Just look how he's made the child cry. I might have known, you bully. It *would* be the son of that disgusting tart. But it's *your* fault, Rosa, *you* teach him to pick on other kids. I was right when I told you yesterday I never want to speak to you again, after that dirty trick you pulled on me!'

'Come on, honey, let's go,' Rosa said to Jaime.

He stood up and went off with Rosa, never looking back.

Raul was still sobbing when they got home. He had a low fever. His mother put him to bed, hovering over him because he was in such a state. The boy took forever getting to sleep.

The next day, after a restless night, his fever and crying continued. They asked him where it hurt, but he wouldn't speak.

Carmen was fired when, frightened at this turn of events,

she confessed everything. As the summer went on, the mother dedicated herself more and more to taking care of her son. The fever dropped and the sobbing diminished. But he still had slight bags under his red eyes. After a week, he was well again and begged his mother to take him down to the beach in the afternoon.

It turned out to be a beautiful afternoon. A slight breeze made him aware of his cheeks and the contours of his arms in the air. The torches of lobelias and bougainvillea burned in hedges and on balconies. The horizon was precise and light, as if drawn with a single stroke of a knife. The sea died peacefully on the beach. Mother and son installed themselves on the hot sand. Antonio, seeing them come down, came over to say hello to his aunt, and then sat down next to his cousin. Raul began to sing softly, and Antonio laughed, until Juana called to him from a distance. Raul thought that perhaps Antonio had been forbidden to play with him. Then he began to play at pouring sand into his sandals, letting it drift out gently through the perforations.

'Your father will be down in a little while. We'll go for a walk, just the three of us . . .' his mother said.

Raul didn't answer. She was smiling and, rare for her, her hair looked nice. But the child didn't see this. He simply knew it. He knew it, just as he knew many things now. He had lost weight and his features had come out with the sharpness of a man's. He had fixed his enormous blue eyes on the horizon. He had hardly spoken since he had got well.

Without turning around, he said to his mother: 'My father's coming down because Jaime left, isn't that true?'

'How do you know they left?'

She helped him begin a mound of sand.

'And that's why you're so happy, right?'

'Yes,' said his mother, who was still a young woman, although somewhat faded. 'His family was bored here.'

The boy said very little during the rest of the summer. His parents were busy with other things and didn't notice. They only noticed how much he'd grown. Sometimes Raul would sing for his cousin Antonio, but the child would pull away: the truth was, he preferred to play horses. Pia said those songs were out of fashion and, besides, she liked songs with words. All of them had clearly defined tastes, they were 'just like real people,' as the grown-ups said. Raul spent the rest of the summer sitting on the sand by himself, humming something nobody recognized. With his eyes fixed on the horizon, he appeared to be looking at somebody, at some thing.

THE 'GÜERO'

As soon as I got off the train at the Veracruz station and stepped into that hot, noisy world, so different from what I was used to, I had the disagreeable premonition that everything was going to go wrong in this scramble of people and objects. And in fact it did, at first, because right on the station platform part of my luggage went astray. Then the cab driver took forever finding the hotel where I was supposed to stay, and once I got there I blew up at the manager because the shower I had anxiously looked forward to during the train ride wouldn't work until the plumber gave it a going over.

Once those initial problems were solved, I went down to the street, and with the idea of drinking something cool I made myself comfortable at a little table in the arcade facing the main square of Veracruz. My uneasiness vanished as if by magic, leaving me astounded at what my senses were discovering. On my trip through the towns of the Mexican plateau, I had been impatient to see the last of them and descend, finally, to the tropics. This was what I was seeing from my table. In a wave my faith came back to me—the faith of those who are very young and know only the temperate zones—that in those places filled with excesses I was sure to have definitive experiences, much richer than the ones I had known. They were within reach, I could almost feel them, just as my fingers were touching the tall, cold glass.

The sun had ceased to glint off the cupola of the immense salmon-colored church on the opposite side of the square. Every afternoon, the clouds opened up over the harbor, carrying in a squall from the Gulf that moistened and burned at the same time. As it got darker, more people came into the square, and soon it was full of bustle and noise. The music of the itinerant marimbas got louder. Girls dressed in loud-colored skirts walked by unhurriedly, encouraging or rebuffing the glances of men dressed in white pants and shirts who were loitering in groups, having their shoes shined or arguing with the vendor about the price of a slice of pineapple. A block away, behind the arcades, the cranes squealed on the docks, loading boats on their way to or from Jamaica and Belize, Mérida and Tampico, Havana and Puerto Limón.

Though it's not in front of the liveliest part of the square, the Café de la Parroquia is the most authentically native gathering place in Veracruz. The city's industrialists and politicians come there in the afternoon, with or without their families, to talk to any acquaintance who's willing and able to waste a little time while sipping something cool. Sallow-skinned hacienda owners come there to see each other too, killing time before the plane takes them to Tabasco, Chiapas, or Quintana Roo. Many North American tourists come to Veracruz, but few of them go to the Café de la Parroquia, because generally they prefer the arcades of the more cosmopolitan hotels on the opposite side of the plaza.

I had heard all this, so I headed for that café as soon as I stepped out of the hotel. But just as I sat down I felt cheated: there it was, the typical, nasal accent of Americans, right at the next table. The occupants were three women. At first glance, there was nothing particularly striking about them since they were well along in years and not much to look at. But just as I got ready to change tables, one of the women caught my attention. She wasn't wearing that pseudo-exotic costume of flowery skirts and barbaric jewelry considered *de rigueur* for a trip to Mexico by so many North American matrons. Her face was nothing but suntanned skin clinging to fine bones crowned by a short crop of gray hair. In the instant our eyes met, she did something strange: she smiled at me. Then perfectly naturally she put on her glasses, reached into a bag for wool and knitting needles, and began to knit without interrupting her conversation. I decided not to change tables and to listen to what she was saying.

She spoke with simplicity and authority about Mexican things, about cities and people and plants. She was a botanist by profession and had lived in Mexico for years. Her companions were tourists who had chanced to meet Mrs. Howland, the lady with gray hair, on their trip.

'Tráeme otra Coca-Cola, güero,' she told the waiter.

'Ahorita, güera,' he answered.

In Mexico, the word *güero* means blond, but as a gesture of friendship one uses it with people who do not obviously have Indian or Negro blood. The waiter was something less than blond, but since his skin wasn't too dark, the word was natural enough. I would have liked to meet Mrs. Howland. That smile and the peacefulness she emanated suggested that she lived and knew things as I would have liked to live and know them.

The boy brought Mrs. Howland's Coca-Cola. Having finished it, she announced it was time to go, because she had to leave early the next morning. Her friends asked her where she was going, and she said to Tlacotlalpan, a town up the Papaloapan River, five hours by launch from Alvarado. She made a few remarks about this old town on the River of the Butterflies, isolated in the middle of the jungle. The images her words evoked in me made everything I saw from my table suddenly look boring: the palm trees in the square, the marimbas in the crowded arcades, the languid smiles that glowed white under pale straw hats—all this was a cheap poster to attract tourists. I was young and very ashamed of looking like a tourist, since I wanted to belong to those chosen few who don't know how to look like tourists. Maybe Mrs. Howland's words had shown me a path.

She smiled at me again as she took off her glasses and put away her knitting. She said goodbye to her companions and I watched her walk away in the rain that had unleashed itself on the city, driving the people out of the square. I went back to the hotel and found out that Alvarado is some kilometers south of Veracruz. I asked to be called early the next morning to catch the bus.

On arrival in Alvarado the first thing I saw was Mrs. Howland. There she was, sitting on her suitcase on the pier, next to the stands of fruit and dried fish. She was amusing herself watching sea turtles being unloaded from the boats. Nobody was paying any attention to her, which seemed curious, since in Mexico strangers are stared at, and this inquisitive-looking woman dressed in khaki pants was well worth a stare. At least she was more peculiar-looking than I—I wasn't much of a spectacle and was dressed very simply, yet many of the townspeople turned as they passed and said with amusement: *'Adiós, güero!'* Maybe I was staring too much, dazzled by the morning's color and movement, and by the view of the open river sluggishly stretching toward the horizon.

The launch pulled in and rapidly filled with passengers, who sat down behind the dirty hemp curtains that hung from the ceiling as a shield against the sun. They were carrying bags of food and drink, and Mrs. Howland sat down in the midst of some country people with bundles and children and baskets.

I climbed up to the roof because I didn't want curtains to impede my view of the landscape. I was sure that my beautiful Veracruz sombrero, with its broad, floppy brim, was enough protection against the brutal sun.

The launch pulled away. I leaned back, resting my head on my knapsack, gazing at the town, while the white houses and stands of palm and mango trees dotting the hills slowly disappeared. Then there was nothing more than a heavy sky, the wounding heat of the humid air, and the uneven dark lines of the river banks. We chugged ahead, leaving a wake that smelled of gas as we skirted the clumps of floating hyacinth.

Mrs. Howland's voice disturbed my reverie. 'Come down at once, young man, or you'll get sunstroke.'

I leaned over the edge of the roof and answered: 'Don't worry, lady, I'm used to the sun. Besides, this hat—'

'Young man,' her impatient voice interrupted, 'not even the people who were born here dare do that. Don't be a fool, come down immediately.'

She made room for me at her feet among the close-packed travelers, and went on knitting something whose shape I couldn't determine, knitting calmly, as if nothing was happening.

'Beer is the thing to beat this heat,' she said abruptly. 'I'm going to have one.'

She asked the attendant to bring two. We drained our bottles and after wiping her mouth, Mrs. Howland said: 'I saw you yesterday in the Café de la Parroquia.'

'Yes, I was there in the afternoon. You gave me the idea of going to Tlacotlalpan . . .'

'You'd never heard of it before?' she asked, taking off her glasses and resting her needles. 'It's a marvelous town that's existed for centuries on the banks of this river and nothing's changed it. It's surrounded by jungle and coconut palm plantations. The only contact with the outside world is this launch and the boats that come during the harvest season to transport the crop.'

'Do you live there?'

'Not any more. I used to. It's years since I've been there. They say nothing's changed.'

'And why hadn't you gone back?' I asked at the risk of seeming nosy.

'My husband died a few months ago and it's only now that I'm free to come. He hated Tlacotlalpan. It was so full of painful memories that he never let me go back. My husband's death finished everything for me. . . . Now I'm returning to see if the town that witnessed the most important event in my life can brighten the years I have left. My husband was a botanist too . . .'

She sat in silence for a few moments, and I could see that in her mind she was trying to organize a variety of ideas and emotions. The curtains near her dark face swayed slightly. Suddenly, as if she had plunged into her past, she sat up straight and threw this question at me: 'Do you know the kind of person who lives according to theories, theories that stipulate the precise name and the exact weight of everything, thereby banishing all possible mystery?'

She seemed to drain herself with the force of her question, because another silence followed. But Mrs. Howland's question repeated itself over and over inside my head, as if the launch were pulling her words along with it. I didn't know what to answer, and I didn't think it was necessary. The tone of her voice was calmer when she continued: 'My husband and I were perfect specimens of that species. We both belonged to rich families and had connections in the best scientific and intellectual circles in our country. We knew each other as classmates at a small but prestigious university. From the moment I met him, I admired Bob. He was the best student in his field, in addition to being tall and blond, very handsome right up until the last. While we were students, we worked together and thought together in perfect harmony. We were convinced that nobody could be more clear-headed, sane, and intelligent than ourselves. Family ties were absurd, race and class prejudice moronic, science was the only thing that mattered, and people in general were boring and vulgar. We got married as soon as we received our Ph.D.'s. We had everything: good looks—now don't laugh, I used to be very pretty—culture, intelligence, health; and, of course, unpleasant surprises didn't fit into the life we had planned so carefully. We were concerned with a certain highly specialized branch of experimental botany. Our theories were novel but scholarly, so the university hired us as assistant professors.

'Do you have any idea what life is like in a small university in the United States? Well, then you know it's the perfect environment for people like us. We worked like maniacs during the day and in the late afternoon we would walk around under the old oak trees and feed bread crumbs to the campus squirrels and wave to students we knew, while we watched the dormitory lights go on one by one. Every once in a while we went to parties, always dressed in our best tweeds. We talked about politics, science, books, or we heard the latest gossip about our tiny world. Once a week our favorite students came for tea, so we could show them we were human beings too.

'Our university life lasted for a few happy years. Then we moved to New York to take better jobs. At first we felt very isolated in that immense city, and our work brought us together more than ever before. But New York is a monster that will devour every last molecule of humility. Bob undertook a huge research project, the results of which weren't appreciated until much later, on a serious, profound, difficult subject, while I let myself be tempted into writing popularizing articles for pseudo-scientific magazines, which made me famous overnight. People thought I was a brilliant woman tied to a gloomy man, a laboratory rat who didn't produce anything. I began to believe this myself and grew bored with my husband. I threw away my provincial academic tweeds for fashionable clothes. It was exciting to see myself dressed up and to watch other people admire me. I became more and more distant from Bob and he from me, but before we made a decisive break, I found out I was pregnant. The child died a week after it was born. With this the distance between us grew, and I threw myself into society life. I was satisfied with my mode of existence, and said that being civilized people, we shouldn't limit our inclinations. I thought I was free because I had thrown all obligations out the window, but underneath it all the idea that I wasn't capable of doing work on the level of Bob's tormented me.

'Nine months after Bob came home drunk one night, I had another child, his son. Around that time the University of Mexico offered Bob a professorship with tenure. I was disoriented, but clinging to the somewhat fictitious tie this son offered us, I went with him. Bob's work was brilliant but meanwhile a dangerous envy pulled me away from him completely, those first ten years in Mexico, and yet I never decided to take any drastic steps.

'To amuse myself in my free time, I suppose, I determined that my son was going to be a great man. From a very early age he was going to reason for himself and act according to his own inclinations, free from any blemish that might warp what was to be the fullest of lives. He was a handsome child. His big eyes were the deepest, most transparent blue I've ever seen, his head was perfectly shaped, and his hair was like silky gold.

'Mike was nine when Bob decided he had to take leave to write a book based on the vast pile of material that had mounted up over years of teaching and research. He needed a quiet place to do it, and a friend of ours said Tlacotlalpan was the answer. The book was to be the chief work of his life, and although I wasn't anxious to bury myself in the jungle with a man I didn't love, I think the vision of the glory his book would bring and the desire not to be excluded from such a great accomplishment enticed me along.

'I think this is the same launch we took when we first went up there, twenty years ago. Although we'd traveled all around Mexico, it was eerie to find an immense cathedral painted ultramarine in a town of two thousand inhabitants lost in the jungle. The tiny streets, on which grass grew, were bordered with solid one-story houses with porches on the street, painted pink, yellow, blue, green. The river flowed silently past the pier, which was made of treetrunks, and on under the banana, mango, and palm trees, carrying along floating islands of blue hyacinths. Coconut plantations, and beyond them the jungle, surrounded the town. In the patios red tulips grew, hanging like lanterns from the bushes that swarmed at night with fireflies. And there were cages with parrots, and women shuffling around in wooden clogs on the cool, polished tile floors.

'Oh, those first days! Remembering that beauty wounds me more than it did when I first laid eyes on it! And Amada Vásquez! That age-old quality in her Indian eyes, that mixture of magic and confused religions and fear. It's one of time's practical jokes that she's still alive and I'm going back to her house as if nothing had happened. That pink patio, that rocking chair in constant motion, those mosquito nets delicate as mist, those sheets stiff with starch and cleanliness, all that still exists. In a few hours I'll see her again. Do you suppose that parrot my son Mike taught English is still alive? It might still be swinging on its perch near the washing place at the private dock on the river behind the house.

'The moment we clambered onto the pier, the people who'd come to meet the launch surrounded us. Seeing Mike, they exclaimed in wonder: *"El güero, el güero!"* One woman passed her dark hand over the boy's golden head. I was proud of him for not being scared.

'My husband used to say he fell in love with Amada Vásquez at first sight. She was minute and brown as a cockroach, and walked very fast with hardly any movement. She was as old as time, her body shrunken, her thin, long braids barely graying, her face wrinkled as the bark of a tree. She rented rooms to select guests. We loved her house so much, we persuaded her to rent the whole place to us, including her personal services. Amada, who was a spinster, made white vestments for the church vestry. I don't know how many times I watched her pulling at her needle, embroidering complicated designs, adding fringes and odds and ends with her dark hands using immaculate pieces of thread. In the thick of the afternoon heat, she would sit on the porch in a rattan rocking chair and everybody who went by smiled respectfully. The house had been given to her by the Lara sisters, two maiden ladies who were very ancient and very pure, as a reward for having dedicated most of her life to their comfort. On Amada's death, the house will go to the parish church.

'It didn't take us long to settle in to Amada's house. Mike adored her from the beginning and followed her around on all her errands. In Mexico City we never sent our son to school because we were afraid he'd pick up prejudices there. We taught him everything we felt he required for a decent education. But he would be ten years old in a few months, and we thought it would be a good idea to send him to public school in Tlacotlalpan, where the town children went. That way he would acquire a sense of justice and equality, which we so much wanted him to have.

'I took him to school a week after we got there. The teacher, Miss Hidalgo, was very honored to have the *güero* among her students. I went with him as far as the classroom. When Mike sat down at one of the empty desks in the middle of the classroom, the teacher ordered a boy in the first row to change seats with him. I wouldn't permit it. I made a special point of telling Miss Hidalgo I didn't want my son treated differently from the other children.

'That's the most beautiful image I have of him. I see him in that classroom, in the middle of those handsome brown boys with restless knowing eyes like black insects, who turned to look at him, while he smiled innocently: he was a different being, perfect, a thing apart.

'When Mike came home that day, I was surprised to see him march straight to his room and take off his shoes.

' "What are you doing?" I asked.

' "The thing is, I'm the only person in school with shoes," he answered. There was humiliation in his voice. "They were picking on me."

' "Did they want to steal them?"

' "No. At first they didn't dare come near me and I was alone all during morning recess. Then they made friends and asked me to lend them my shoes to try on . . ."

'Mike said they felt his hair and one of the more daring ones had tried to stick a finger in his eye to touch the blue. All of this made me uncomfortable. However quaint it might be to see my son go barefoot to a public school in a town in the middle of the jungle, I couldn't permit it. I explained to the boy that we were different, that the people of our race were more delicate because we weren't used to the climate, unlike his schoolmates. But Mike insisted on going to school barefoot. For the same reason, I explained, we drank only boiled water, for example, and prepared our food differently. It took a lot of patience to convince him his feet wouldn't tolerate the rough ground or the hot tiles at midday.

'The next day I didn't see Mike go out. You can imagine my surprise when just after noon, while I was chatting with Amada on the porch, I saw the teacher come around the corner, carrying Mike and followed by a group of children.

'I ran to meet them. Miss Hidalgo said she thought it had been our idea to send Mike to school with no shoes on. The child was crying in her arms, his feet cut and bruised. Classes had been called off and most of the students had come along to bring the *güero* home.

'I demanded an explanation from Mike. He said at school

they had dared him to walk across the burning tiles in the patio, and then on a patch of thistles. This had been the result. I complained to Miss Hidalgo, and she assured me it wouldn't happen again.

'As time went on, the boy grew more and more addicted to following Amada around everywhere. Often I heard them talking in the next room, and afterwards Mike would come and ask what I thought of the stories the old woman was telling him. They were stories about miraculous birds and animals, about good gods that protected the world and lived at the source of the river. But something strange happened: as he became fonder of these stories, he stopped telling them to me. But I still liked to see them together. Doing the wash at the riverside, Amada stooped and stood up, stooped and stood up, always talking to Mike, who sat beside her on the dock and splashed water with his feet.

'From the moment we got to Tlacotlalpan, what most fascinated Mike was the boats. And he was right. They were magical, those colorful boats: they rocked while tied to the dock day after day; and at dusk, under the sky that was red when there wasn't a storm, they brought home the workers who had been laboring on the opposite bank; and some had heeled over under the roots of the enormous mango trees and looked like tired animals taking refuge in the shade. Mike went to the pier a lot, and the Santelmo brothers went with him. They were healthy, handsome boys, and I cultivated their friendship for my son because they weren't servile like Ramírez, who had been the first friend Mike made in Tlacotlalpan. I also encouraged Mike's interest in boats, to get him away from Amada, who was beginning to trouble me.

'She worried me for a number of reasons. At first I thought this woman's admiration for our material advantages, like that of all the townpeople's, was unconditional, but as time went on I realized the admiration wasn't pure, that an unknown element was spoiling it.

'I remember one afternoon, coming home from a visit to the parish priest whom we had befriended, I heard voices in my room. I looked inside, and you can imagine my astonishment at finding Amada dressed in one of my skirts, imitating my mannerisms in front of two friends who were doubled over with laughter. My boxes were in a mess and my things were strewn across the floor. Amada's imitation was perfect. She mimicked my way of walking and in my usual tone of voice mumbled words that were meant to be English. Blushing to see myself so cruelly caricatured, I went inside and ordered her to put the things away. To keep her from getting angry I gave her the skirt she had on, and she was delighted.

'After that, our belongings began to disappear, especially Mike's toys. I asked him about it and he didn't know what to say. I left it at that, since so much as a word against Amada would send him into a fit of rage. I attributed the disappearances to the covetousness of our landlady. But the loss of those cheap objects didn't matter; the advantages of living in her house were too great.

'One night Mike woke up crying, and Bob and I ran to his bedside. He murmured a series of incoherent things and went back to sleep. But the nightmares grew more frequent. He would wake up screaming, sobbing, begging Amada to come to him. He carried on about rivers, treasures, gods, stormy nights, but it didn't worry me too much. I attributed it to the change of environment. Nonetheless, I kept an eye on our landlady, who had filled him with the fairy tales that were upsetting the level-headedness I wanted him to acquire.

'Time went on and Bob did nothing but write. The book was growing. But the work I was doing for the book was so useless I couldn't help coming to think that I just wasn't suited to such work. It pained me to admit science no longer interested me. Bob interested me even less. We decided to get a separation when we went back, and I simply couldn't wait for him to write the final paragraph. The only thing that gave me any pleasure was watching Mike. He adapted admirably to the environment and made many friends among his schoolmates. At first, being timid in school, Mike chose timid friends. Then his shyness turned into daring, and he chose daring friends. These boys played games that were so intense, so serious, that I couldn't help feeling there was something dangerous about them.

'One afternoon Miss Hidalgo paid a call on me. It was very difficult to get her to tell me exactly what was the matter, but after much beating around the bush she confessed she couldn't control Mike any more. He had incited a group of his schoolmates to rebel. If the *güero* said he wasn't going to school, they would wander with him around the plantations, the jungle, and the river. If Mike refused to do his homework, the rest of them did the same. Sometimes, using what the spinster called ostentatious gifts, he got the more industrious students to do his homework for him. This, and not what I had suspected, was the reason so many objects had disappeared from his room. I was ashamed to remember the number of times I had asked him about them, while he pretended such perfect innocence that I believed him. Miss Hidalgo stayed all afternoon, telling me things about Mike. For example, it seemed that the *güero* told certain stories to his friends, stories that were kept a deep secret. Often she saw him squatting in a corner of the patio with a group of boys around him. This group were the chosen, who went around with their heads held high, and the ones who didn't belong tried to ingratiate themselves with the *güero* to get in.

'I thought these were a spinster's exaggerations. In any case I scolded Mike for not telling me the truth about the disappearance of his toys. He pleaded with me not to get mad. He said it was natural for him to want to give his toys away because they were extraordinary things to his friends, while he didn't care one way or the other about them.

'One morning, going to the door with my son to send him off to school I saw at least ten schoolmates waiting for him across the street. I found this disquieting, after what Miss Hidalgo had told me. When Mike came home that afternoon, I interrogated him.

'"It's just that they admire me," he answered.

'"Admire you?" I said in astonishment. "You must be a very good student. You must have done something very important."

'"No, it's not that. It's just that they know I'm different."

'"Different?"

'"Yes, different." Then he added in a defiant tone: "You yourself told me so when the thing about the shoes happened."

'I didn't know what attitude to take. Was this the result of all my theories and intentions? I gave him a good dressing down. It was too difficult to explain things to a ten-year-old child, and I no longer had the strength to do anything but think about our return to civilization. Silently I sat darning a sock under the lamp, while insects buzzed around it. Mike was flipping through a book and glancing at the door from time to time. Amada had gone out. She would be back soon to serve our dinner. Mike suddenly said:

'"Amada says the same thing and Miss Hidalgo thinks it and tells everybody else . . ."

'Apparently he wanted to start an argument. I was afraid and refused to say anything but: "This must stop immediately."

'He persisted: "Then you never heard what happened between Ramírez' mother and the Santelmos' mother? That's very funny. Everybody in town knows about it. Remember how I was that idiot Ramírez' friend in the beginning and then I got bored with him and made friends with the Santelmos? Well, the two families live next door to each other. When I made friends with the Santelmos and didn't want to mess around with Ramírez any more, the two families had a fight. Now they won't speak to each other. They say one day Ramírez' mother bumped into Mrs. Santelmo on the dock and pushed her into the water and she almost drowned. . . ."

'The tone of his story terrified me so that I didn't dare raise my eyes from my darning. I pretended to be incredulous.

'"And why do they like you so much? You must be a very good little boy. . . ."

'Hearing that, Mike looked at me with the most disturbing expression I have ever seen in the eyes of a child. It was laughter mingled with the most profound contempt for my simplemindedness. I felt as if I were talking to a being much older and infinitely wiser than I was. My son had acquired a dimension I could not control.

'"Yes, that's why . . ." he answered.

'"And that's all?"

'Just then Amada arrived. Mike went off with her and I didn't dare stop him.

'I tried to explain my fears to Bob, but he didn't understand, because all he could think about was the book he was finishing. He said it was pointless to worry, since we were leaving in less than a month. Furthermore, I didn't understand what was going on myself. But while Bob worked, I had plenty of time to worry about Mike. The boy had two personalities: with Bob and me, he was polite, unsmiling, and devious; he always seemed to be thinking about something else. On the other hand, when he was with Amada or the Santelmos, he was ebullient and daring. His nightmares now were very frequent, and he would sometimes say during them that far away, at the river's source, the powerful golden-haired gods lived, and anyone who reached their dwelling place would be their equal. He spoke of a bird that lighted up the forest with its golden plumage; he spoke of Amada and boat rides at night up the river.

'Miss Hidalgo complained again that she couldn't do anything with Mike: nobody went to school, they all followed him on his jaunts. I couldn't control him either. I mutely watched the change take place in him during our stay in Tlacotlalpan, through contact with so many primitive forces, with Amada, with those children whose eyes understood the ancient vocabulary of the jungle and the river. Mike himself was like a river whose banks had overflowed with the rains. All those forces seemed to have poured themselves into my son, and, being blind, I wasn't aware that he was too delicate to stand it. I say blind, because I thought contact with Mike would provide those children with a civilizing influence, since he was a superior being not only to me, but to them too. I didn't know that they and everything around them had stretched Mike's life to the point that whatever was mysterious and vibrant with hidden life had come to be his natural element.

'All afternoon one day, a black wind blew, disturbing the smoothness of the sky, and that night the heavy clouds burst into lightning and rain, swallowing the town and the roaring river and the swollen jungle in a vast pocket of unbreathable heat. It was one of many hot squalls we'd had in Tlacotlalpan, so we didn't think twice about going to Father Hilario's, where we had been invited to dine. Passing the dock we saw that all the boats except one had been drawn out of the water to protect them from the storm. The one remaining creaked as it was tossed by the waves, and since we didn't know to whom it belonged, we couldn't warn its owner to save it from its certain fate.

'Father Hilario's cook, who liked us very much, had prepared our favorite dishes. After much food and much talking, we were about to leave, when we heard the screams of a child at the door. I turned white and ran to open it. The wind gusted into the house, and on the threshold I saw little Ramírez staring at me. He was soaking wet, trembling and speechless. I instantly understood that what had been brewing all during our stay in Tlacotlalpan had happened. After that, my memories of that night are confused. But much later, from the same boy who had shouted at Father Hilario's door, and who had been part of the game up until the last moment, I found out how it happened.

'That night, it seems, when we left and Amada went to her room, Mike got dressed to go out. I will never know, and I prefer not to, whether it happened with Amada's consent. I'd rather believe it didn't.

'Today I close my eyes and I can imagine the whole thing. Mike runs through the streets' sodden grass, and the rain pours down on that golden head of a small god whom the elements do not inconvenience. At a corner on the square he joins his companions and they run off to the dock. Seeing the black sky shattered by rays of lightning, feeling the hot wind whipping the waves and treetops into motion, Ramírez, who in spite of everything still belongs to the group, begins to falter. It seems he couldn't stand the idea that not he but Pedro Santelmo was Mike's lieutenant, and jealousy, or terror, made him think twice. Ramírez told me Mike used to repeat Amada's stories to his friends, especially that story about the golden-haired gods who live at the source of the river and how you had to go there on a stormy night to be their equal. Mike convinced them that if they went with him, they would acquire all their powers, riches, and wisdom. Ramírez said the expedition had been planned for a long time. The chief chose only ten companions. I can imagine what promises my son made to get those children, the sons of people who feared the river from knowing it too well, to come with him on that broken-down old boat. Did he promise them gold? Or to be different, like him? Or to have the superhuman knowledge they gave him credit for? I don't know . . .

'From the dock, Ramírez watched them get in the boat. I cannot imagine how ten boys, from ten to twelve years old, managed to do it on such a windy night. Where did they get the strength? Where did they get the courage? I don't know . . . Ramírez watched them try to control the boat, blinded by the stinging rain, while Mike insulted them for hesitating to get aboard. Mike shouted for them to set the boat loose, they took up oars, and with him at the tiller they lurched into the turbulent river.

'They had a small lantern with them. I can imagine their faces around it in the rain, next to that feeble light, I can see my son's face, serious and intense, holding the tiller. I imagine the savage determination on the face of each one of those boys. I imagine the impotence, the anger at their impotence. I imagine the tiny boat with its feeble light jumping on the black waves of the furious river. From the middle of the river they would see the handful of lights marking the town on one bank, and on the other, the fastnesses of blind, hot vegetation, glimpsed in the lightning. I would like to imagine—it's some consolation at least—that the enthusiasm for their game lasted at least a few minutes, that their faith in the adventure achieved greatness in the few moments before terror took control of them, when they heard the boat creak and begin to come apart, before the thunder of wind and water drowned out their cries for help, before the boat foundered, before the waters of the river, infuriated at this sacrilege of ten children who dared defy it, closed over their heads. . . .'

Toward the end of the story, Mrs. Howland's voice took on the brilliance and precision of a jewel in that hot air which seemed to dissolve everything, except for the quality of her voice and words. I watched her hands, still knitting, and I thought I perceived the shape and object of that knitting. I watched her head against the dirty curtains: it was eternal, wise, dark—probably like the face of Amada Vásquez.

'The rescue,' she went on, her voice almost expressionless, 'took all night. The entire town, including ourselves, gathered at the dock, with storm lanterns and flashlights that did no good in that vast darkness. Bob and some other fathers spent the night searching the river in a boat. I don't know how he didn't die too, but I wasn't afraid when I watched him get on board. The whole thing was futile. They didn't find a trace of the children. I later heard that after several days two bodies were found near the mouth of the river. But neither of them was Mike.

'We left the town as soon as we could. I hated that ill-omened town, those unfortunate people. But slowly time put together some semblance of order inside me, and I found a new love for work, and for Bob, and for people. I had time to think a lot and to draw a line—for lack of a better way to say it—around what happened. But not a line that separated it from my life and from the rest of human experience. . . .'

Her voice hung suspended in the silence for a long while.

I asked her to climb up on the roof of the launch to watch the landing, but I don't think she heard me, so intent was she on her knitting. I stood on the roof and let the hot air bathe my face. I closed my eyes and opened them again: it was as if I was seeing for the first time.

We were approaching the green line of the river bank, now speckled with movement and the different greens of different trees. From time to time we passed small piers, houses supported on stilts over the water, men with bare chests and white hats moving from the shade into the sunlight. A bird shrieked in the jungle: the note of its cry rose long and clear, gathering all other noises into it. Afterwards there was a silence. Beyond some treetops and roofs, I saw the blue towers of the church of Tlacotlalpan.

I don't know how long I stood there, looking at it. Later I remembered Mrs. Howland's warning about the sun. I climbed down, asked for a beer, and waited for the launch to dock. Seeing me disembark, the town children cried out at me:

'Güero! Güero! Güero!'

A LADY

FOR MARTHA GIBERT

I DON'T remember exactly when I first became aware of her existence. But if I'm not mistaken, it was a certain winter afternoon on a streetcar going through a poor district.

When I tire of my room and my usual conversations, I have a habit of taking any streetcar that comes along, without knowing its route, and touring like that through the city. That afternoon I brought along a book, just in case I felt like reading, but I never opened it. It was raining on and off and the streetcar was almost empty. I sat next to a window, wiping the steam off the glass so I could look out at the streets.

I don't remember the exact moment she sat down beside me. But when the streetcar stopped at a corner, a sensation ordinary and at the same time mysterious invaded me: what I was seeing, that exact moment, unimportant as it was, I had experienced before, or perhaps I had dreamed it. The scene seemed just like another that I had already known: in front of me, a reddish neck poured in folds over a threadbare shirt collar; three or four persons were scattered throughout the empty streetcar; outside, in the darkness that had fallen in the last few minutes, there was a corner drugstore with its brightly lit sign, and a military policeman yawning beside the red mailbox. I also noticed a knee covered by a green raincoat, next to my knee.

I recognized the sensation, and instead of disturbing me it pleased me. So I didn't rack my brain to figure out where and when all this had happened before. I smiled ironically to myself, dissipating the sensation, and only glanced to see what was connected to that knee covered with a green raincoat.

It was a lady. A lady with a wet umbrella in her hand and a functional hat on her head. One of those fifty-odd-year-old ladies of whom there are thousands in this city: neither handsome nor ugly, neither rich nor poor. Her regular features showed the remains of a rather banal kind of good looks. Her eyebrows grew closer together than most women's over her nose: that was the most distinctive thing about her face.

I make this description in the light of later events, because what I observed of the lady at the time was very little. The bell clanged and the streetcar lurched on, causing the familiar scene to disappear, and I returned to watching the street through the hole I had wiped on the window. The streetlights lit up. A boy came out of a store with two carrots and a roll in his hand. A row of squat houses stretched out along the sidewalk: window, door, two windows; while the cobblers, gas fitters, and greengrocers shut down their tiny shops.

I was so distracted that I didn't notice when my neighbor got off the streetcar. Why should I have noticed, since after the instant in which I glanced at her I didn't give her another thought?

I didn't give her another thought until the next night.

I live in a neighborhood very different from the one the streetcar had taken me through the previous afternoon. There are trees along the sidewalks and the houses are half hidden behind iron fences and hedges. It was rather late and I was tired, since I had spent a good part of the evening chatting with friends over beer and cups of coffee. I was walking home with my collar pulled up. Before crossing the street I spotted a familiar-looking figure moving off under the darkness of the trees. I stopped to watch for a moment. Yes. It was the woman who sat next to me in the streetcar the previous afternoon. When she passed beneath a streetlamp I immediately recognized her green raincoat. There must be thousands of green raincoats in this city, but I never doubted it was hers, remembering it in spite of having seen her for only a few seconds, during which nothing about her had impressed me. I crossed to the other side. That night, I fell asleep without thinking about the figure moving off under the trees on the lonely street.

One sunny morning, a couple of days later, I saw the lady on an avenue downtown. The noontime bustle was at its peak. Women were stopping in front of shop windows, chattering about buying a dress or a piece of material. The men were coming out of their offices with documents under their arms. Again I recognized her, seeing her go by as part of all this, even though she wasn't dressed as she had been on the other occasions. I was slightly puzzled: why hadn't her identity erased itself from my mind and become confused with the rest of the city's inhabitants?

From then on, I began to see the lady very frequently. I found her everywhere, at all hours. But sometimes a week or more would go by without my seeing her. I was struck by the melodramatic thought that perhaps she was following me. But I discarded the idea when I realized that unlike myself, she did not recognize me in the middle of the crowds. I, on the other hand, enjoyed discovering her face among so many unknown features. I would sit on a park bench, and she would cross the park carrying a bag full of vegetables. I would stop to buy a pack of cigarettes, and there she was, paying for hers. I would go to the movies, and the lady would be sitting two seats over. She didn't look at me, but I amused myself by watching her. She had rather thick lips. She wore a large ring that was somewhat vulgar.

After a while, I began to look for her. The day didn't seem complete without seeing her. Reading a book, for example, I caught myself making conjectures about the lady instead of concentrating on the print. I placed her in imaginary situations, in the midst of objects I didn't know. I began to gather facts about her, all of which were lacking in importance and meaning. She liked the color green. She only smoked a certain brand of cigarettes. She was the one who bought food for her household.

Sometimes I felt such a need to see her that I would drop whatever I was meant to be doing and go out to look for her. And sometimes I found her. Sometimes I didn't, and I would return in a filthy humor to lock myself in my room, unable to think of anything else the rest of the night.

One day I went out for a walk. On my way home, as it was getting dark, I sat down on a bench in one of the squares. Only in this city are there squares like these. Small and new, it seemed to be an accident in that utilitarian neighborhood, which was neither rich nor poor. The trees were flimsy, as if they refused to grow, offended at being planted in such poor soil, in an area so gloomy and dull. On one corner, a soda machine lit up the shapes of three boys talking to each other in the middle of the blob of light. Inside a dry fountain, which apparently had never been finished, there were broken tiles, fruit peels, crumpled paper. Couples were sitting on the other benches but hardly spoke to one another, as if the ugliness of the square was not conducive to greater intimacy.

Along one of the paths I saw the lady coming, arm in arm with another woman. They spoke agitatedly but walked slowly. As they passed in front of me, I heard the lady say, in an anguished tone: 'Impossible!'

The other woman put her arm around the lady's shoulders to console her. Skirting the dry fountain, they moved off down another path.

Uneasy, I stood up and went off in hopes of finding them, to ask the lady what had happened. But they had disappeared, while a few people hurried by on the last errands of the day.

I had no peace all week after this incident. I walked around the city, hoping the lady would cross my path, but I didn't see her. She seemed to have obliterated herself, and I abandoned my various activities. I no longer had the least power of concentration. I had to see her go by, nothing more, to know if the pain of that afternoon in the square was still with her. I lingered around the places I had usually seen her, and even thought about stopping some people who looked as if they might be her relatives or friends to ask about her. But I wouldn't have known whom to ask for and I let them go by. I didn't see her all that week.

The weeks that followed were worse. I went so far as to pretend I was sick, so that I could stay in bed and forget that presence who was filling my thoughts. Perhaps after a few days of not going out, I would find her right off the bat, and when I least expected to. But I couldn't control myself, and after two days in which the lady never once left my room, I went out. When I got up, I felt weak, physically ill. Even so, I rode the streetcar, I went to the movies, I searched the grocery store, I watched an outdoor circus. The lady simply wasn't anywhere.

But after some time, I saw her again. I was leaning over to tie my shoelace and I saw her walking along the sunny sidewalk across the street, smiling broadly and carrying a mimosa branch, one of the first in bloom that season. I wanted to follow her, but she disappeared in the confusion of streets.

Her image vanished from my mind after losing her that time. I went back to my friends, I met people, and I walked around, alone or with others, in the streets. It wasn't that I forgot her. Rather, her presence had fused with the rest of the people who live in the city.

One morning, some time afterward, I woke up with the certainty that the lady was dying. It was Sunday, and after lunch I went out for a walk under the trees in my neighborhood. On a balcony, an old lady was basking in the sun, her knees covered with a fuzzy blanket. A girl was painting garden furniture red on her lawn, getting it ready for summer. There were few people around, and the objects and noises sketched themselves sharply in the clean air. But somewhere in the same city where I was walking, the lady was about to die.

I went home and installed myself in my room to wait.

From my window I watched the electricity wires vibrate in the breeze. The afternoon grew older beyond the roofs, and behind the hills the light waned. The wires kept on vibrating, breathing. In the garden, somebody was watering the grass with a hose. The birds were getting ready for night, filling all the treetops I could see from my window with noise and movement. A child laughed in the garden next door. A dog barked.

Suddenly, all the noises stopped at once, and a well of silence opened up in the peaceful afternoon. The wires stopped vibrating. In an unknown neighborhood, the lady had died. A certain house would have its door set ajar that night, and candles would burn in a room full of quiet voices and comfortings. The afternoon slipped away toward an imperceptible end, and all my thoughts about the lady were extinguished. Afterwards, I must have fallen asleep, because I don't remember anything else about the afternoon.

The next day I saw in the newspaper that the bereaved family of Doña Ester de Arancibia announced her passing, and gave the time and place of the funeral service. Could it be? Yes. Doubtless it was she.

I went to the interment, following the cortège slowly through the long avenues, behind silent people who knew the features and the voice of the woman for whom they were mourning. Afterwards I walked home, because that sunny afternoon brought me a special tranquillity.

Now I only think about the woman from time to time, in the afternoon.

Sometimes I am struck by the idea that, on a corner for example, the present scene is nothing more than the reproduction of another, lived once before. On these occasions it occurs to me that I am going to see the lady walk by, with her eyebrows that grow together and her green raincoat. But it makes me laugh a little, because with my own eyes I saw her coffin deposited in a niche, in a wall with hundreds of other niches exactly like it.

THE WALK

FOR MABEL CARDAHI

I

IT HAPPENED when I was very small, when my Aunt Matilde and Uncle Gustavo and Uncle Armando, my father's unmarried sister and brothers, and my father himself, were still alive. Now they are all dead. That is, I'd rather think they are all dead, because it's easier, and it's too late now to be tortured with questions that were certainly not asked at the opportune moment. They weren't asked because the events seemed to paralyze the three brothers, leaving them shaken and horrified. Afterwards, they erected a wall of forgetfulness or indifference in front of it all so they could keep their silence and avoid tormenting themselves with futile conjectures. Maybe it wasn't that way; it could be that my imagination and my memory play me false. After all, I was only a boy at the time, and they weren't required to include me in their anguished speculations, if there ever were any, or keep me informed of the outcome of their conversations.

What was I to think? Sometimes I heard the brothers talking in the library in low voices, lingeringly, as was their custom; but the thick door screened the meaning of the words, allowing me to hear only the deep, deliberate counterpoint of their voices. What were they saying? I wanted them to be talking in there about what was really important; to abandon the respectful coldness with which they addressed one another, to open up their doubts and anxieties and let them bleed. But I had so little faith that would happen; while I loitered in the high-walled vestibule near the library door, the certainty was engraved on my mind that they had chosen to forget, and had come together only to discuss, as always, the cases that fell within their bailiwick, maritime law. Now I think perhaps they were right to want to erase it all, for why should they live with the useless terror of having to accept that the streets of a city can swallow a human being, annul it, leave it without life or death, suspended in a dimension more threatening than any dimension with a name?

And yet . . .

One day, months after the incident, I surprised my father looking down at the street from the second-floor sitting room. The sky was narrow, dense, and the humid air weighed on the big limp leaves of the ailanthus trees. I went over to my father, anxious for some minimal explanation.

'What are you doing here, father?' I whispered.

When he answered, something closed suddenly over the desperation on his face, like a shutter slamming on an unmentionable scene.

'Can't you see? I'm smoking,' he answered.

And he lit a cigarette.

It wasn't true. I knew why he was looking up and down the street, with his eyes saddened, once in a while bringing his hand up to his soft brown goatee: it was in hopes of seeing her reappear, come back just like that, under the trees along the sidewalk, with the white dog trotting at her heels. Was he waiting there to gain some certainty?

Little by little I realized that not only my father but both his brothers, as if hiding from one another and without admitting even to themselves what they were doing, hovered around the windows of the house, and if a passerby chanced to look up from the sidewalk across the street, he might spot the shadow of one of them posted beside a curtain, or a face aged by suffering in wait behind the window panes.

2

YESTERDAY I passed the house we lived in then. It's been years since I was last there. In those days the street under the leafy ailanthus trees was paved with quebracho wood, and from time to time a noisy streetcar would go by.

Now there aren't any wooden pavements, or streetcars, or trees along the sidewalk. But our house is still standing, narrow and vertical as a book slipped in between the thick shapes of the new buildings; it has stores on the ground floor and a loud sign advertising knit undershirts stretched across the two second-floor balconies.

When we lived there, most of the houses were tall and slender like ours. The block was always cheerful, with children playing games in the splashes of sunlight on the sidewalks, and servants from the prosperous homes gossiping as they came back from shopping. But our house wasn't happy. I say 'wasn't happy' as opposed to 'was sad,' because that's exactly what I mean. The word 'sad' wouldn't be correct because it has connotations that are too clearly defined; it has a weight and dimensions of its own. And what went on in our house was exactly the opposite: an absence, a lack, which, because it was unknown, was irremediable, something that had no weight, yet weighed because it didn't exist.

When my mother died, before I turned four, they thought I needed to have a woman around to care for me. Because Aunt Matilde was the only woman in the family and lived with my uncles Gustavo and Armando, the three of them came to our house, which was big and empty.

Aunt Matilde carried out her duties toward me with the punctiliousness characteristic of everything she did. I didn't doubt that she cared for me, but I never experienced that affection as something palpable that united us. There was something rigid about her feelings, as there was about those of the men in the family, and love was retained within each separate being, never leaping over the boundaries to express itself and unite us. Their idea of expressing affection consisted of carrying out their duties toward one another perfectly, and above all, of never upsetting one another. Perhaps to express affection otherwise was no longer necessary to them, since they shared so many anecdotes and events in which, possibly, affection had already been expressed to the saturation point, and all this conjectural past of tenderness was now stylized in the form of precise actions, useful symbols that did not require further explanation. Respect alone remained, as a point of contact among four silent, isolated relatives who moved through the halls of that deep house which, like a book, revealed only its narrow spine to the street.

I, of course, had no anecdotes in common with Aunt Matilde. How could I, since I was a boy and only half understood the austere motives of grown-ups? I desperately wanted this contained affection to overflow, to express itself differently, in enthusiasm, for example, or a joke. But she could not guess this desire of mine because her attention wasn't focused on me. I was only a peripheral person in her life, never central. And I wasn't central because the center of her whole being was filled with my father and my uncles Gustavo and Armando. Aunt Matilde was the only girl—an ugly girl at that—in a family of handsome men, and realizing she was unlikely to find a husband, she dedicated herself to the comfort of those men: keeping house for them, taking care of their clothes, preparing their favorite dishes. She carried out these functions without the slightest servility, proud of her role because she had never once doubted her brothers' excellence and dignity. In addition, like all women, she possessed in great measure that mysterious faith in physical well-being, thinking that if it is not the main thing, it is certainly the first, and that not to be hungry or cold or uncomfortable is the prerequisite of any good of another order. It wasn't that she suffered if defects of that nature arose, but rather that they made her impatient, and seeing poverty or weakness around her, she took immediate steps to remedy what she did not doubt were mere errors in a world that ought to be—no, *had* to be—perfect. On another plane, this was intolerance of shirts that weren't ironed exquisitely, of meat that wasn't a prime cut, of dampness leaking into the humidor through someone's carelessness. Therein lay Aunt Matilde's undisputed strength, and through it she nourished the roots of her brothers' grandness and accepted their protection because they were men, stronger and wiser than she.

Every night after dinner, following what must have been an ancient family ritual, Aunt Matilde went upstairs to the bedrooms and turned down the covers on each one of her brothers' beds, folding up the bedspreads with her bony hands. For him who was sensitive to the cold, she would lay a blanket at the foot of the bed; for him who read before going to sleep, she would prop a feather pillow against the headboard. Then, leaving the lamps lit on the night tables beside their vast beds, she went downstairs to the billiard room to join the men, to have coffee with them and play a few caroms before they retired, as if by her command, to fill the empty effigies of the pajamas laid out on the neatly turned-down white sheets.

But Aunt Matilde never opened my bed. Whenever I went up to my room I held my breath, hoping to find my bed turned down with the recognizable expertise of her hands, but I always had to settle for the style, so much less pure, of the servant who did it. She never conceded me this sign of importance because I was not one of her brothers. And not to be 'one of my brothers' was a shortcoming shared by so many people . . .

Sometimes Aunt Matilde would call me in to her room, and sewing near the high window she would talk to me without ever asking me to reply, taking it for granted that all my feelings, tastes, and thoughts were the result of what she was saying, certain that nothing stood in the way of my receiving her words intact. I listened to her carefully. She impressed on me what a privilege it was to have been born the son of one of her brothers, which made it possible to have contact with all of them. She spoke of their absolute integrity and genius as lawyers in the most intricate of maritime cases, informing me of her enthusiasm regarding their prosperity and distinction, which I would undoubtedly continue. She explained the case of an embargo on a copper shipment, another about damages resulting from a collision with an insignificant tugboat, and another having to do with the disastrous effects of the overlong stay of a foreign ship. But in speaking to me of ships, her words did not evoke the magic of those hoarse foghorns I heard on summer nights when, kept awake by the heat, I would climb up to the attic and watch from a roundel the distant lights floating, and those darkened blocks of the recumbent city to which I had no access because my life was, and always would be, perfectly organized. Aunt Matilde did not evoke that magic for me because she was ignorant of it; it had no place in her life, since it could not have a place in the life of people destined to die with dignity and then establish themselves in complete comfort in heaven, a heaven that would be identical to our house. Mute, I listened to her words, my eyes fixed on the length of light-colored thread which, rising against the black of her blouse, seemed to catch all the light from the window. I had a melancholy feeling of frustration, hearing those foghorns in the night and seeing that dark and starry city so much like the heaven in which Aunt Matilde saw no mystery at all. But I rejoiced at the world of security her words sketched out for me, that magnificent rectilinear road which ended in a death not feared, exactly like this life, lacking the fortuitous and unexpected. For death was not terrible. It was the final cutoff, clean and definite, nothing more. Hell existed, of course, though not for us, but rather to punish the rest of the city's inhabitants, or those nameless sailors who caused the damages that, after the struggle in the courts was over, always filled the family bank accounts.

Any notion of the unexpected, of any kind of fear, was so alien to Aunt Matilde that, because I believe fear and love to be closely related, I am overcome by the temptation to think that she didn't love anybody, not at that time. But perhaps I am wrong. In her own rigid, isolated way, it is possible that she was tied to her brothers by some kind of love. At night, after dinner, when they gathered in the billiard room for coffee and a few rounds, I went with them. There, faced with this circle of confined loves which did not include me, I suffered, perceiving that they were no longer tied together by their affection. It's strange that my imagination, remembering that house, doesn't allow more than grays, shadows, shades; but when I evoke that hour, the strident green of the felt, the red and white of the billiard balls, and the tiny cube of blue chalk begin to swell in my memory, illuminated by the hanging lamp that condemned the rest of the room to darkness. Following one of the many family rituals, Aunt Matilde's refined voice would rescue each of her brothers from the darkness as his turn came up: 'Your shot, Gustavo . . .'

And cue in hand, Uncle Gustavo would lean over the green of the table, his face lit up, fragile as paper, the nobility of it strangely contradicted by his small, close-set eyes. When his turn was over, he retreated into the shadows, where he puffed on a cigar whose smoke floated lackadaisically off, dissolved by the darkness of the ceiling. Then their sister would say: 'Your shot, Armando . . .'

And Uncle Armando's soft, timid face, his great blue eyes shielded by gold-framed glasses, would descend into the light. His game was generally bad, because he was the 'baby,' as Aunt Matilde sometimes called him. After the comments elicited by his game, he would take refuge behind the newspaper and Aunt Matilde would say: 'Pedro, your shot . . .'

I held my breath watching my father lean over to shoot; I held it seeing him succumb to his sister's command, and, my heart in a knot, I prayed he would rebel against the established order. Of course, I couldn't know that that rigid order was in itself a kind of rebellion invented by them against the chaotic, so that the terrible hand of what cannot be explained or solved would never touch them. Then my father would lean over the green felt, his soft glance measuring the distances and positions of the balls. He would make his play and afterwards heave a sigh, his moustache and goatee fluttering a little around his half-open mouth. Then he would hand me his cue to chalk with the little blue cube. By assigning me this small role, he let me touch at least the periphery of the circle that tied him to his brothers and sister, without letting me become more than tangential to it.

Afterwards Aunt Matilde played. She was the best shot. Seeing her ugly face, built up it seemed out of the defects of her brothers' faces, descend into the light, I knew she would win; she had to win. And yet . . . didn't I see a spark of joy in those tiny eyes in the middle of that face, as irregular as a suddenly clenched fist, when by accident one of the men managed to defeat her? That drop of joy was because, although she might want to, she could never have *let* them win. That would have been to introduce the mysterious element of love into a game which should not include it, because affection had to remain in its place, without overflowing to warp the precise reality of a carom.

3

I NEVER liked dogs. Perhaps I had been frightened by one as a baby, I don't remember, but they have always annoyed me. In any case, at that time my dislike of animals was irrelevant since we didn't have any dogs in the house; I didn't go out very often, so there were few opportunities for them to molest me. For my uncles and father, dogs, as well as the rest of the animal kingdom, did not exist. Cows, of course, supplied the cream that enriched our Sunday dessert brought in on a silver tray; and birds chirped pleasantly at dusk in the elm tree, the only inhabitant of the garden behind our house. The animal kingdom existed only to the extent that it contributed to the comfort of their persons. It is needless to say, then, that the existence of dogs, especially our ragged city strays, never even grazed their imaginations.

It's true that occasionally, coming home from Mass on Sunday, a dog might cross our path, but it was easy to ignore it. Aunt Matilde, who always walked ahead with me, simply chose not to see it, and some steps behind us, my father and uncles strolled discussing problems too important to allow their attention to be drawn by anything so banal as a stray dog.

Sometimes Aunt Matilde and I went early to Mass to take communion. I was almost never able to concentrate on receiving the sacrament, because generally the idea that she was watching me without actually looking at me occupied the first plane of my mind. Although her eyes were directed toward the altar or her head bowed before the Almighty, any movement I made attracted her attention, so that coming out of church, she would tell me with hidden reproach that doubtless some flea trapped in the pews had prevented my concentrating on the thought that we shall all meet death in the end and on praying for it not to be too painful, for that was the purpose of Mass, prayer, and communion.

It was one of those mornings.

A fine mist was threatening to transform itself into a storm, and the quebracho paving extended its neat glistening fan shapes from sidewalk to sidewalk, bisected by the streetcar rails. I was cold and wanted to get home, so I hurried the pace under Aunt Matilde's black umbrella. Few people were out because it was early. A colored gentleman greeted us without tipping his hat. My aunt then proceeded to explain her dislike of persons of mixed race, but suddenly, near where we were walking, a streetcar I didn't hear coming braked loudly, bringing her monologue to an end. The conductor put his head out the window: 'Stupid dog!' he shouted.

We stopped to look. A small white bitch escaped from under the wheels, and, limping painfully with its tail between its legs, took refuge in a doorway. The streetcar rolled off.

'These dogs, it's the limit the way they let them run loose . . .' protested Aunt Matilde.

Continuing on our way, we passed the dog cowering in the doorway. It was small and white, with legs too short for its body and an ugly pointed nose that revealed a whole genealogy of alleyway misalliances, the product of different races running around the city for generations looking for food in garbage cans and harbor refuse. It was soaking wet, weak, shivering with the cold or a fever. Passing in front of it, I witnessed a strange sight: my aunt's and the dog's eyes met. I couldn't see the expression on my aunt's face. I only saw the dog look at her, taking possession of her glance, whatever it contained, merely because she was looking at it.

We headed home. A few paces further on, when I had almost forgotten the dog, my aunt startled me by turning abruptly around and exclaiming: 'Shoo, now! Get along with you!'

She had turned around completely certain of finding it following us and I trembled with the unspoken question prompted by my surprise: 'How did she know?' She couldn't have heard it because the dog was following us at some distance. But she didn't doubt it. Did the glance that passed between them, of which I had only seen the mechanical part —the dog's head slightly raised toward Aunt Matilde, Aunt Matilde's head slightly turned toward it—did it contain some secret agreement, some promise of loyalty I hadn't perceived? I don't know. In any case, when she turned to shoo the dog, her voice seemed to contain an impotent desire to put off a destiny that had already been accomplished. Probably I say all this in hindsight, my imagination imbuing something trivial with special meaning. Nevertheless, I certainly felt surprise, almost fear, at the sight of my aunt suddenly losing her composure and condescending to turn around, thereby conceding rank to a sick, dirty dog following us for reasons that could not have any importance.

We arrived home. We climbed the steps and the animal stayed down below, watching us through the torrential rain that had just begun. We went inside, and the delectable smell of a post-communion breakfast erased the dog from my mind. I had never felt the protectiveness of our house so deeply as I did that morning; the security of those walls delimiting my world had never been so delightful to me.

What did I do the rest of the day? I don't remember, but I suppose I did the usual thing: read magazines, did homework, wandered up and down the stairs, went to the kitchen to ask what was for dinner.

On one of my tours through the empty rooms—my uncles got up late on rainy Sundays, excusing themselves from church —I pulled a curtain back to see if the rain was letting up. The storm went on. Standing at the foot of the steps, still shivering and watching the house, I saw the white dog again. I let go of the curtain to avoid seeing it there, soaking wet and apparently mesmerized. Suddenly, behind me, from the dark part of the sitting room, Aunt Matilde's quiet voice reached me, as she leaned over to touch a match to the wood piled in the fireplace: 'Is she still there?'

'Who?'

I knew perfectly well who.

'The white dog.'

I answered that it was. But my voice was uncertain in forming the syllables, as if somehow my aunt's question was pulling down the walls around us, letting the rain and the inclement wind enter and take over the house.

4

THAT MUST have been the last of the winter storms, because I remember quite vividly that in the following days the weather cleared and the nights got warmer.

The white dog remained posted at our door, ever trembling, watching the window as though looking for somebody. In the morning, as I left for school, I would try to scare it away, but as soon as I got on the bus, I saw it peep timidly around the corner or from behind a lamppost. The servants tried to drive it away too, but their attempts were just as futile as my own, because the dog always came back, as if to stay near our house was a temptation it had to obey, no matter how dangerous.

One night we were all saying good night to one another at the foot of the stairs. Uncle Gustavo, who always took charge of turning off the lights, had taken care of all of them except that of the staircase, leaving the great dark space of the vestibule populated with darker clots of furniture. Aunt Matilde, who was telling Uncle Armando to open his window to let some air in, suddenly fell silent, leaving her good nights unfinished. The rest of us, who had begun to climb the stairs, stopped cold.

'What's the matter?' asked my father, coming down a step.

'Go upstairs,' murmured Aunt Matilde, turning to gaze into the shadows of the vestibule.

But we didn't go upstairs.

The silence of the sitting room, generally so spacious, filled up with the secret voice of each object—a grain of dirt slipping down between the old wallpaper and the wall, wood creaking, a loose window pane rattling—and those brief seconds were flooded with sounds. Someone else was in the room with us. A small white shape stood out in the shadows near the service door. It was the dog, who limped slowly across the vestibule in the direction of Aunt Matilde, and without even looking at her lay down at her feet.

It was as if the dog's stillness made movement possible for us as we watched the scene. My father came down two steps, Uncle Gustavo turned on the lights, Uncle Armando heavily climbed the stairs and shut himself into his room.

'What is this?' my father asked.

Aunt Matilde remained motionless.

'How could she have got in?' she asked herself suddenly.

Her question seemed to imply a feat: in this lamentable condition, the dog had leaped over walls, or climbed through a broken window in the basement, or evaded the servants' vigilance by slipping through a door left open by accident.

'Matilde, call for somebody to get it out of here,' my father said, and went upstairs followed by Uncle Gustavo.

The two of us stood looking at the dog.

'She's filthy,' she said in a low voice. 'And she has a fever. Look, she's hurt . . .'

She called one of the servants to take her away, ordering her to give the dog food and call the veterinarian the next day.

'Is it going to stay in the house?' I asked.

'How can she go outside like that?' Aunt Matilde murmured. 'She has to get better before we can put her out. And she'll have to get better quickly, because I don't want any animals in the house.' Then she added: 'Get upstairs to bed.'

She followed the servant who was taking the dog away.

I recognized Aunt Matilde's usual need to make sure everything around her went well, the strength and deftness that made her the undoubted queen of things immediate, so secure inside her limitations that for her the only necessary thing was to correct flaws, mistakes not of intention or motive, but of state of being. The white dog, therefore, was going to get well. She herself would take charge of that, because the dog had come within her sphere of power. The veterinarian would bandage the dog's foot under her watchful eyes, and, protected by gloves and a towel, she herself would undertake to clean its sores with disinfectants that would make it whimper. Aunt Matilde remained deaf to those whimpers, certain, absolutely certain, that what she was doing was for the dog's good.

And so it was.

The dog stayed in the house. It wasn't that I could see it, but I knew the balance between the people who lived there, and the presence of any stranger, even if in the basement, would establish a difference in the order of things. Something, something informed me of its presence under the same roof as myself. Perhaps that something was not so very imponderable. Sometimes I saw Aunt Matilde with rubber gloves in her hand, carrying a vial full of red liquid. I found scraps of meat on a dish in a basement passageway when I went down to look at a bicycle I had recently been given. Sometimes, the suspicion of a bark would reach my ears faintly, absorbed by floors and walls.

One afternoon I went down to the kitchen and the white dog came in, painted like a clown with the red disinfectant. The servants threw it out unceremoniously. But I could see it wasn't limping anymore, and its once droopy tail now curled up like a plume, leaving its hindquarters shamelessly exposed.

That afternoon I said to Aunt Matilde: 'When are you going to get rid of it?'

'What?' she asked.

She knew perfectly well what I meant.

'The white dog.'

'She's not well yet,' she answered.

Later on, I was about to bring up the subject again, to tell her that even if the dog wasn't completely well yet, there was nothing to prevent it from standing on its hind legs and rooting around in the garbage pails for food. But I never did, because I think that was the night Aunt Matilde, after losing the first round of billiards, decided she didn't feel like playing anymore. Her brothers went on playing and she, sunk in the big leather sofa, reminded them of their turns. After a while she made a mistake in the shooting order. Everybody was disconcerted for a moment, but the correct order was soon restored by the men, who rejected chance if it was not favorable. But I had seen.

It was as if Aunt Matilde was not there. She breathed at my side as always. The deep, muffling rug sank as usual under her feet. Her hands, crossed calmly on her lap—perhaps more calmly than on other evenings—weighed on her skirt. How is it that one feels a person's absence so clearly when that person's heart is in another place? Only her heart was absent, but the voice she used to call her brothers contained new meanings because it came from that other place.

The next nights were also marred by this almost invisible smudge of her absence. She stopped playing billiards and calling out turns altogether. The men seemed not to notice. But perhaps they did, because the matches became shorter, and I noted that the deference with which they treated her grew infinitesimally.

One night, as we came out of the dining room, the dog made its appearance in the vestibule and joined the family. The men, as usual, waited at the library door for their sister to lead the way into the billiard room, this time gracefully followed by the dog. They made no comment, as if they hadn't seen it, and began their match as on other nights.

The dog sat at Aunt Matilde's feet, very quiet, its lively eyes examining the room and watching the players' maneuvers, as if it was greatly amused. It was plump now, and its coat, its whole body glowed, from its quivering nose to its tail, always ready to wag. How long had the dog been in the house? A month? Longer, perhaps. But in that month Aunt Matilde had made it get well, caring for it without displays of emotion, but with the great wisdom of her bony hands dedicated to repairing what was damaged. Implacable in the face of its pain and whimpers, she had cured its wounds. Its foot was healed. She had disinfected it, fed it, bathed it, and now the white dog was whole again.

And yet none of this seemed to unite her to the dog. Perhaps she accepted it in the same way that my uncles that night had accepted its presence: to reject it would have given it more importance than it could have for them. I saw Aunt Matilde tranquil, collected, full of a new feeling that did not quite overflow to touch its object, and now we were six beings separated by a distance vaster than stretches of rug and air.

It happened during one of Uncle Armando's shots, when he dropped the little cube of blue chalk. Instantly, obeying a reflex that linked it to its picaresque past in the streets, the dog scampered to the chalk, yanked it away from Uncle Armando who had leaned over to pick it up, and held it in its mouth. Then a surprising thing happened. Aunt Matilde, suddenly coming apart, burst out in uncontrollable guffaws that shook her whole body for a few seconds. We were paralyzed. Hearing her, the dog dropped the chalk and ran to her, its tail wagging and held high, and jumped on her skirt. Aunt Matilde's laughter subsided, but Uncle Armando, vexed, left the room to avoid witnessing this collapse of order through the intrusion of the absurd. Uncle Gustavo and my father kept on playing billiards; now more than ever it was essential not to see, not to see anything, not to make remarks, not even to allude to the episode, and perhaps in this way to keep something from moving forward.

I did not find Aunt Matilde's guffaws amusing. It was

only too clear that something dark had happened. The dog lay still on her lap. The crack of the billiard balls as they collided, precise and discrete, seemed to lead Aunt Matilde's hand first from its place on the sofa to her skirt, and then to the back of the sleeping dog. Seeing that expressionless hand resting there, I also observed that the tension I had never before recognized on my aunt's face—I never suspected it was anything other than dignity—had dissolved, and a great peace was softening her features. I could not resist what I did. Obeying something stronger than my own will, I slid closer to her on the sofa. I waited for her to beckon to me with a look or include me with a smile, but she didn't, because their new relationship was too exclusive; there was no place for me. There were only those two united beings. I didn't like it, but I was left out. And the men remained isolated, because they had not paid attention to the dangerous invitation to which Aunt Matilde had dared to listen.

5

COMING HOME from school in the afternoon, I would go straight downstairs and, mounting my new bicycle, would circle round and round in the narrow garden behind the house, around the elm tree and the pair of iron benches. On the other side of the wall, the neighbors' walnut trees were beginning to show signs of spring, but I didn't keep track of the seasons and their gifts because I had more serious things to think about. And as I knew nobody came down to the garden until the suffocations of midsummer made it essential, it was the best place to think about what was happening in our house.

Superficially it might be said nothing was happening. But how could one remain calm in the face of the curious relationship that had arisen between my aunt and the white dog? It was as if Aunt Matilde, after punctiliously serving and conforming to her unequal life, had at last found her equal, someone who spoke her innermost language, and as among women, they carried on an intimacy full of pleasantries and agreeable refinements. They ate bonbons that came in boxes tied with frivolous bows. My aunt arranged oranges, pineapples, grapes on the tall fruit stands, and the dog watched as if to criticize her taste or deliver an opinion. She seemed to have discovered a more benign region of life in this sharing of pleasantries, so much so that now everything had lost its importance in the shadow of this new world of affection.

Frequently, when passing her bedroom door, I would hear a guffaw like the one that had dashed the old order of her life to the ground that night, or I would hear her conversing—not soliloquizing as when talking to me—with someone whose voice I could not hear. It was the new life. The culprit, the dog, slept in her room in a basket—elegant, feminine, and absurd to my way of thinking—and followed her everywhere, except into the dining room. It was forbidden to go in there, but waited for its friend to emerge, followed her to the library or the billiard room, wherever we were going, and sat beside her or on her lap, and from time to time, sly looks of understanding would pass between them.

How was this possible? I asked myself. Why had she waited until now to overflow and begin a dialogue for the first time in her life? At times she seemed insecure about the dog, as if afraid the day might come when it would go away, leaving her alone with all this new abundance on her hands. Or was she still concerned about the dog's health? It was too strange. These ideas floated like blurs in my imagination while I listened to the gravel crunching under the wheels of my bicycle. What was not blurry, on the other hand, was my vehement desire to fall seriously ill, to see if that way I too could gain a similar relationship. The dog's illness had been the cause of it all. Without that, my aunt would never have become linked to it. But I had an iron constitution, and furthermore it was clear that inside Aunt Matilde's heart there was room for only one love at a time, especially if it were so intense.

My father and uncles didn't seem to notice any change at all. The dog was quiet, and abandoning its street manners it seemed to acquire Aunt Matilde's somewhat dignified mien; but it preserved all the impudence of a female whom the vicissitudes of life have not been able to shock, as well as its good temper and its liking for adventure. It was easier for the men to accept than reject it since the latter would at least have meant speaking, and perhaps even an uncomfortable revision of their standards of security.

One night, when the pitcher of lemonade had already made its appearance on the library credenza, cooling that corner of the shadows, and the windows had been opened to the air, my father stopped abruptly at the entrance to the billiard room.

'What is this?' he exclaimed, pointing at the floor.

The three men gathered in consternation to look at a tiny round puddle on the waxed floor.

'Matilde!' Uncle Gustavo cried.

She came over to look and blushed with shame. The dog had taken refuge under the billiard table in the next room. Turning toward the table, my father saw it there, and suddenly changing course he left the room, followed by his brothers, heading toward the bedrooms, where each of them locked himself in, silent and alone.

Aunt Matilde said nothing. She went up to her room followed by the dog. I stayed in the library with a glass of lemonade in my hand, looking out at the summer sky and listening, anxiously listening to distant foghorns and the noise of the unknown city, terrible and at the same time desirable, stretched out under the stars.

Then I heard Aunt Matilde descend. She appeared with her hat on and her keys jingling in her hand.

'Go to bed,' she said. 'I'm taking her for a walk on the street so she can take care of her business there.'

Then she added something that made me nervous: 'The night's so pretty . . .'

And she went out.

From that night on, instead of going upstairs after dinner to turn down her brothers' beds, she went to her room, put on her hat, and came down again, her keys jingling. She went out with the dog, not saying a word to anybody. My uncles and my father and I stayed in the billiard room, or, as the season wore on, sat on the benches in the garden, with the rustling elm and the clear sky pressing down on us. These nightly walks of Aunt Matilde's were never mentioned, there was never any indication that anybody knew anything important had changed in the house; but an element had been introduced there that contradicted all order.

At first Aunt Matilde would stay out at most fifteen or twenty minutes, returning promptly to take coffee with us and exchange a few commonplaces. Later, her outings inexplicably took more time. She was no longer a woman who walked her dog for reasons of hygiene; out there in the streets, in the city, there was something powerful attracting her. Waiting for her, my father glanced furtively at his pocket watch, and if she was very late, Uncle Gustavo went up to the second floor, as if he had forgotten something there, to watch from the balcony. But they never said anything. Once when Aunt Matilde's walk had taken too long, my father paced back and forth along the path between the hydrangeas, their flowers like blue eyes watching the night. Uncle Gustavo threw away a cigar he couldn't light satisfactorily, and then another, stamping it out under his heel. Uncle Armando overturned a cup of coffee. I watched, waiting for an eventual explosion, for them to say something, for them to express their anxiety and fill those endless minutes stretching on and on without the presence of Aunt Matilde. It was half past twelve when she came home.

'Why did you wait up for me?' she said smiling.

She carried her hat in her hand and her hair, ordinarily so neat, was disheveled. I noted that daubs of mud stained her perfect shoes.

'What happened to you?'

'Nothing,' was her answer, and with that she closed forever any possible right her brothers might have had to interfere with those unknown hours, happy or tragic or insignificant, which were now her life.

I say they were her life, because in those instants she remained with us before going to her room, with the dog, muddy too, next to her, I perceived an animation in her eyes, a cheerful restlessness like the animal's, as if her eyes had recently bathed in scenes never before witnessed, to which we had no access. These two were companions. The night protected them. They belonged to the noises, to the foghorns that wafted over docks, dark or lamplit streets, houses, factories, and parks, finally reaching my ears.

Her walks with the dog continued. Now she said good night to us right after dinner, and all of us went to our rooms, my father, Uncle Gustavo, Uncle Armando, and myself. But none of us fell asleep until we heard her come in, late, sometimes very late, when the light of dawn already brightened the top of our elm tree. Only after she was heard closing her bedroom door would the paces by which my father measured his room stop, and a window be closed by one of her brothers to shut out the night, which had ceased being dangerous for the time being.

Once after she had come in very late, I thought I heard her singing very softly and sweetly, so I cracked open my door and looked out. She passed in front of my door, the white dog cuddled in her arms. Her face looked surprisingly young and perfect, although it was a little dirty, and I saw there was a tear in her skirt. This woman was capable of anything; she had her whole life before her. I went to bed terrified that this would be the end.

And I wasn't wrong. Because one night shortly afterwards, Aunt Matilde went out for a walk with the dog and never came back.

We waited up all night long, each one of us in his room, and she didn't come home. The next day nobody said anything. But the silent waiting went on, and we all hovered silently, without seeming to, around the windows of the house, watching for her. From that first day fear made the harmonious dignity of the three brothers' faces collapse, and they aged rapidly in a very short time.

'Your aunt went on a trip,' the cook told me once, when I finally dared to ask.

But I knew it wasn't true.

Life went on in our house as if Aunt Matilde were still living with us. It's true they had a habit of gathering in the library, and perhaps locked in there they talked, managing to overcome the wall of fear that isolated them, giving free rein to their fears and doubts. But I'm not sure. Several times a visitor came who didn't belong to our world, and they would lock themselves in with him. But I don't believe he had brought them news of a possible investigation; perhaps he was nothing more than the boss of a longshoremen's union who was coming to claim damages for some accident. The door of the library was too thick, too heavy, and I never knew if Aunt Matilde, dragged along by the white dog, had got lost in the city, or in death, or in a region more mysterious than either.

THE CLOSED DOOR

ADELA DE RENGIFO often complained that destiny had dealt her all the blows of life: she had been widowed at twenty-five, she was poor and had to work to support herself with some dignity, and she had a sickly little son—well, not actually sickly, but weak, one of those children who sleep twice as much as normal children.

In fact, from the time he was born, Sebastián had slept a lot. He closed his eyes as soon as his head touched the pillow his mother had embroidered with such care, and in a second he was sleeping angelically.

'He's such a good and quiet child, the poor thing,' his mother would say to the women at the office. 'He doesn't wake up crying in the middle of the night like most children.'

Adela and Sebastián lived in two rooms on the second floor of a slightly damp and dark boarding house. The rooms weren't too bad, although the windows opened on a light well. When Adela went to work in the morning, Mrs. Mechita, the landlady, took care of Sebastián. But since the child was so quiet, he didn't need much care; he never bothered anybody with the noise and games with which other five-year-olds make life impossible. As soon as Mrs. Mechita began her morning chores, Sebastián would slip back to his room, climb into bed and sleep like a log. Mrs. Mechita would go look at him, because it gave her 'a funny feeling' that a boy of his age liked to sleep instead of amusing himself with things that were more . . . well, more normal. One afternoon, deciding it was her duty to point out the boy's peculiarity to Adela, she played the innocent, and never raising her eyes from the crocheting that always kept her freckled fingers busy, said: 'That child's quite the one for sleeping, isn't he, Adelita! Is he ill?'

Adela answered, very stiffly: 'What's so odd about a child sleeping when he feels like it?'

'Well, it was just a remark . . .' Mrs. Mechita replied. When Adela left, Mrs. Mechita set her mastiff-like jaw, reflecting that young widows were too high-strung and in the future she would be careful not to take another into her boarding house.

Mrs. Mechita's remark mirrored Adela's own anxieties, and she couldn't put it out of her mind. It was a fact that Sebastián slept too much. It wasn't that he was half asleep all day long, but that suddenly, for no good reason, he seemed to feel it would be nice to sleep for a while, and so he did, like a person concentrating on a highly amusing hobby, curled up on his small bed with brass bars or sitting on a chair. Uneasy, his mother would sometimes watch him sleep. This quieted her fears, because surely nothing bad could happen to a being who slept with such a blissful face, as if behind his eyelids scenes from a magical life were floating by.

But much as she tried not to get upset, Adela could not deny that Sebastián was different. How could she help feeling uncomfortable? Different and solitary, he didn't seem to have any connection with what happened around him, neither to people nor things, nor to cold nor heat, nor the constant winter rain splashing on the dust-covered glass of the vestibule skylight. Like the moon, Sebastián only showed half of himself to the world. It was a little frightening. The other boarders were kind to him, more than anything else to please Adela, who was a respectable lady even though she had had a tough life. But she didn't fool herself: she knew nobody liked Sebastián. It did pain her soul, but she knew they were partly right, because it was too odd that a child of five slept so much and didn't like to do anything else. It wasn't that he dozed off because he was sleepy or tired; instead, picking the right time, he would start in sleeping, the way ordinary children start in playing marbles or singing. He didn't have playmates his own age. Books, magazines, and movies bored him. He didn't like to play games. The only thing he seemed to want to do was give up everything and curl up in his bed and sleep.

One day Adela asked him: 'What do you dream about, Sebastián?'

'Do I dream?'

'Yes, don't you see visions when you're asleep, like people or stories?'

Sebastián patted his mother's hands while answering. 'No, I guess not. I don't remember . . .'

Adela was exasperated. 'Then why do you sleep so much if you don't get anything out of it?'

'It's just that I like to, mama . . .'

Hearing this, Adela got really angry. She was obliged to work and sacrifice herself to support him. She was still young and pretty, and yet for her son's sake she didn't accept the propositions of the men who were after her in the office. For his sake, for his sake . . . thousands of deprivations and sorrows, while he indulged himself in the pleasure of sleeping all day long. And he slept because he liked to, for no other reason. She regretted having allowed Sebastián to develop the habit of doing things just because he felt like it: it was a dangerous attitude, immoral even. In the beginning, she had to admit, she obscurely intuited some mysterious function in her son's sleeping, as if those dreams held a treasure, something that, although neither he nor she understood it, might reveal itself in the future as something useful or important. This vague hope had kept her silent with some trepidation. But if it was just a whim, it was indecent! She had her whims too and would have been glad to indulge them.

'Well, mama,' said Sebastián, intimidated by his mother's fit of temper, 'if you want me to, I'll sleep only at night.'

Adela's heart stopped, as if she were on the verge of falling into a well. After a long pause, she asked him in a very serious and deliberate voice: 'Then it's something you do when you want, just because? You can control it?'

'Yes, I sleep when I feel like sleeping . . .'

And seeing her son standing in front of her, so strange, dedicated to something neither of them understood, gazing at her with his poor, serious blue eyes, she felt love overflow inside her and she couldn't stop hugging and kissing him and squeezing him hard against her body.

'No, no, baby,' she said. 'You just sleep as much as you want.'

She reflected bitterly that Sebastián was the spitting image of his father, handsome, but perhaps a little on the slow side. At least he wasn't as smart as Carlos Zauze, her department head at the office, who never gave up trying and was always asking her out and making passes at her; he was respectful enough, but temptingly persistent. Nobody who was all there could enjoy anything as colorless, as substanceless as constant sleep. Well, anyway, next year when he started school she would find out soon enough how intelligent her son was.

At school, Sebastián was, if not brilliant, at least diligent. Docile and quiet, he did what he was asked to do, but not so much as to make himself conspicuous. He did everything in an impersonal way, so that people would leave him alone and he wouldn't have to associate with classmates or teachers. He never went out with friends on holidays. In the afternoon, when school was over, the other children, dusty and tired, would stop to buy candy and make a little mischief before breaking up for the day. But Sebastián went straight home, had tea, and did his homework, thereby earning the right to do as he pleased. Then he would lie down to sleep as if unwilling to waste another second. Saturdays and Sundays he did the same thing. He slept from sunrise to sunset, knowing his behavior and report card prevented Adela's saying anything about it.

Adela sometimes went into his bedroom to watch her son sleeping. There she was unnerved by her old fear—and by an even more serious and disturbing element: respect. She sensed there was something in his sleeping that eluded her, something too big or too subtle to be caught in the small, rather limited net of her imagination. The most disturbing thing was that Sebastián always smiled in his sleep—not the ordinary, reassuring smile of a child dreaming about houses and cars and nice things, and feeling watched over by a beautiful mommy and a powerful daddy. No. This was different. It was as if his spirit left his body to dwell in a wonderful world hidden behind his eyelids. His whole being seemed to be there, inside his sleep, leaving nothing outside to comfort his lonely, watchful mother. There was an almost savage intensity about it, giving the impression that Sebastián's dreaming was complete in itself, powerfully closed, self-sufficient, needing none of the people or the things of the world, including her. She was a shadow that could easily be excluded from any pleasure. For Adela, to watch him sleep was to intuit, cruelly and confusingly, everything she had never been nor ever could be nor ever would understand. And when Sebastián came to be fifteen or sixteen, he seemed to have left his mother so far behind that he could hardly make her out, like a meaningless dot an instant before vanishing at the end of the road.

At this time, Adela, in her early forties, could not continue resisting the advances of Carlos Zauze, who had been after her for so many long years. It was her last chance and she had to take it because she couldn't go on withering away in a cold room at Mrs. Mechita's boarding house. She went out for meals and walks with her admirer, they went to dances and movies together, and for a time Adela was blissful with this life and its new joys. After two months, Zauze asked her to marry him. She happily said yes, and immediately they became lovers. While her son dreamed vague improbabilities in the adjacent room, Adela's dreams were filled with a ticklish moustache and the warmth of masculine legs next to her own. She was not lonely anymore; she was no longer cut off from life by the mysterious diffidence of her son. However, once Carlos Zauze's love was consummated, it slowly waned. Marriage was mentioned less frequently. Tears flowed. Then, perhaps because of the tears, love was mentioned less frequently, until finally they hardly ever saw each other and it became clear that the boss's attention had turned elsewhere, toward a secretary in the personnel department two floors down, a young blonde who was very forward, or so her co-workers informed her.

It took her a while to get over Zauze, but nobody could say she lost her composure. It was too bad she had already told Sebastián she was getting married and was going to give him a new father. Now she was in the uncomfortable position of having to tell him that destiny had destroyed that illusion too.

'Don't you have anything to say?' asked Adela when she realized her confidences didn't upset her son. 'Stop playing with that bottle of salad oil, you'll stain your clothes. I suppose you think your clothes don't cost money?'

Blowing her nose, she added: 'You don't care what happens to me.'

'Yes I do, mama,' Sebastián answered. 'How can you think I don't?'

Adela, sobbing, said: 'No you don't. I'm nothing to you. You're a selfish boy and I'm sick and tired of having to work and live alone. I must be getting old. Yesterday I had to order a pair of glasses because the eye doctor told me I'm far-sighted.'

At this, she began crying again.

'Mama, please don't cry. Here, blow your nose. We've already talked about your job. I finish school this year and I'll get a good job. I want to make money and support you. Besides, I'm almost seventeen and want to enjoy myself too.'

Adela stopped crying suddenly and glared at him. 'But the only thing you enjoy is sleep, like a cretin!'

Now Sebastián looked at his mother and she froze: it was as if he did not see her. Her heart stopped: in that glance she discerned all the incomprehensible and elusive things about her son's life, and again she burst into tears. However, through tears and lamentations, she managed to ask him, for the first time, what his sleeping meant. If she didn't ask him now, she would never again be able to, and she couldn't go on living surrounded by so much dryness, so much loneliness.

'How can I tell you when *I* don't understand?' he answered serenely. Adela, no calmer, shifted the lampshade so the pink light would bathe her son's face, leaving her own in the shadows. 'It's as if I had been born with this gift for sleeping as much as I want, whenever I want. And maybe because it's so easy for me, it's the only thing I like to do. It's as though everything else was shadow and didn't matter. But I've never really understood what's wrong with me. For me, every possible happiness lies in sleeping, this act that seems so poor and absurd, but I was born to do it and it's the only thing that matters to me. I have the feeling that I dream and am happy, that I dream about something real and magical, like a world of light that will make everything clear, not just for me, but, through me, for all people. But when I wake up, I feel a door has closed on the things I dreamed, shutting me off from them, keeping me from remembering what was in the dream, and that door will not allow me to bring the happiness of the dream world back to this life, to this reality in which other people live. I need to open that door. And that's why I have to sleep so much, until I tear that door down, until I remember the happiness in my dream. One day perhaps . . .'

'But, son, you must be crazy, the only people who can do that are the ones who die—'

'No, mama, not die. The dead don't dream. You have to be alive to dream, that's why I have to go on living. I haven't dedicated my entire life to sleeping, but sometimes I feel I ought to even though I don't know what I'm going to find behind that door. I may discover that giving up living like other people was a mistake, that finding out what was behind the door wasn't worth the trouble. But I don't care. The fact that I'm living for a genuine purpose justifies my life and makes sense of it. I think of other people's lives and I pity them because they lack that core I have, because they don't experience the fever that drives me. And if what's behind that door turns out to be what I think, if there is light, if there is something that will allow understanding, and at the same time will explain . . .'

The year after, Sebastián got a job and his mother quit hers. Adela had aged greatly. It was as if seeing Sebastián tired her terribly, as if thinking about him squeezed her dry. She felt destiny had been hard on her, had demanded too much from her, had given her very little in exchange. She consoled herself by playing cards with Mrs. Mechita and calling up her former co-workers from time to time to hear what was going on at the office. With her modest pension and Sebastián's salary, they had enough to get along, and they went on living in the same rooms at the boarding house, with potted ferns set in the middle of immaculate doilies, and the smell of moth-eaten plush curtains.

At the office Sebastián didn't say much to his colleagues. He felt that to make friends, start any relationship that wasn't purely formal, would be to betray his vocation for sleep. He was rather tall and thin and seemed to be made of a fragile and transparent substance different from flesh. This gave him such an interesting appearance that while the girls in the office were powdering their noses or correcting imaginary defects in their hair-dos, they would watch him and giggle, regretting he was so young. He had strange blue eyes that were very pretty.

'The eyes of a saint,' one of the girls said.

'Or an artist,' said another.

'No, the eyes of a great lover,' corrected the boldest of them.

But when Sebastián responded to any of their questions or jibes, his manner was so calm and pleasant, so serene and pure, that they felt defeated, as if he saw them as mere empty shells. They quit teasing him, and Sebastián managed to assume the role of an efficient shadow, letting his silence show that he was a bird of a different feather, that he had neither the time nor the inclination for that kind of game.

The department boss, Aquiles Marambio, who was only ten years older than Sebastián, took him under his wing. Since Marambio talked a great deal and was only interested in listening to himself, he wasn't aware that Sebastián paid no attention to what he was saying. He would sit down beside him and address long harangues to him.

'You've got a great future in this organization, Rengifo, because I'm a good judge of character and I know you're a very serious and capable fellow. Guess how many calculators they sent us from North America? Gorgeous, brand-new machines. The only thing they can't do is talk. Can't you guess? Eighty! Can you imagine what we can do with eighty calculators? Well, I'd say we can do just about anything, anything at all. Don't you agree?'

Aquiles Marambio was short and slight, with a tiny, sparse, black moustache and gold-rimmed glasses. Although he wore dark suits pinched at the waist, he was beginning to show a pot belly; his pointed chin was already doubling up and quaked like a child about to cry whenever anybody disobeyed his instructions or committed some offense against hygiene or punctuality.

Once, after much insistence from his boss, Sebastián accepted an invitation to dine at his house. Seating himself at the table, Aquiles Marambio unfolded his napkin, stuffing two of its corners into his vest pockets, and settled in to wait for dinner, extolling the joys of having one's own house, one's own wife, one's own radio and washing machine. Meanwhile his wife, without parting her lips, displayed an approving smile like a person who holds up a defensive weapon; her heart was not at the dinner table but in the kitchen, and she was praying to God the new cook wouldn't let the roast burn.

After much beating around the bush, Aquiles cleared his throat. 'See here, Rengifo, there is something I want to talk to you about.'

'Yes?'

'Yes,' Marambio answered. After a pause he went on: 'Look, the thing is this. Everybody at the office thinks highly of you because you're efficient and polite. But, you know, in an office the main thing is team spirit. We should work as a family. Otherwise it's impossible to be efficient. People like you, but I have to tell you frankly that they're beginning to wonder about you. They think you're strange, stuck-up. They invite you to parties and outings, they ask you to have a drink or go to the movies, and you've never once accepted. Can you tell me why not?'

'It's just that I almost never go out.'

'But why? At your age you ought to go out and have a good time. You're risking your future for nothing. Why don't you go out more?'

'My mother is all by herself. I have to keep her company.'

'That's no reason. I'm sure if she realized how important it is for you to be sociable, she wouldn't care if she had to sit at home alone a couple of nights a month. That's all it would have to be. I'm telling you this as a friend and a man of experience.'

'Well, the truth is, I'm very lazy. I love sleeping. I'd rather sleep than go out.'

'Don't tell me you spend Saturdays and Sundays asleep!'

'I know it sounds odd, but I do. I am a very sleepy person.'

Aquiles' face suddenly contorted with laughter and he raised his napkin to his mouth to keep from spewing food. 'Did you hear, Sara? Did you hear what this fool said? The great Rengifo's chief amusement is sleeping. I never heard of such a thing. He doesn't go out, he doesn't drink, and he doesn't like women. It's like an addiction.'

'Quite so,' said Sebastián, giggling along with his boss's loud guffaws.

'I've heard of all sorts of vices—Don Juans, junkies, drunkards, and God knows what else—but I swear I never heard of anybody with an addiction for sleep. You're crazy, man! If you sleep all the time, life is going to slip away from you. You have to *live,* man! Look at me!'

Sebastián felt so uncomfortable and guilty that he had no choice but to attempt a vague explanation: 'It's just that I think I'm going to discover something important in my dreams, something more important than . . . well, than living.'

'What if it takes you your whole life to find out, and you die first? It means that you wasted your whole life sleeping and didn't get a thing out of it.'

'I think what I'm going to find will be so marvelous that I'm prepared to take the risk.'

'To risk waking up dead one fine day and having people throw you away, just like that, unused? Oh no, no, never. That's insane. You have to live.'

The conversation began to lag. Just for something to say, Aquiles proposed: 'I'll make you a bet you're going to die without seeing anything.'

Laughing, Sebastián replied: 'Well, if I win, you pay for my funeral.'

Aquiles didn't hesitate to accept.

'And if you win, what do you want?' Sebastián asked.

Aquiles slapped Sebastián on the shoulder and said: 'If I win, I'll send you to a pauper's grave. How's that?'

'Fair enough.'

They shook hands to seal the bargain.

'But how will we know who won?' asked Aquiles, beginning to have his doubts.

'I think when you see my face it will be enough. You'll know.'

'You really are insane.'

Both of them laughed. As he said good night to his protégé, Aquiles advised him: 'It seems to me that what you need is more energy, vitality. Why don't you do exercises like me? I bought some weights and chest expanders, and every morning I do calisthenics. That way you might get enough energy to have fun and go out with women.'

It was more or less the same idea his mother had timidly suggested in desperation at her son's refusal of any kind of amusement, even moviegoing. Whenever she succeeded in persuading him to take her there, in the dark he would fall asleep instantly. Adela was aging rapidly, and every day her sight and hearing grew weaker. It was as though all her faculties were slowly turning off and dissolving. She had suffered so much! Her sufferings were her favorite topic of conversation with Mrs. Mechita, whose freckled fingers now lacked their former dexterity with crochet needles, but she showed an increasing interest in listening to other people's woes.

Once Adela told her son, as if Mrs. Mechita had said it,

what she herself thought: 'Mrs. Mechita, who loves you so much because she's known you almost since you were born, said it seems to her you're wasting your life, that you ought to have some fun, take a vacation this summer, for instance. She said you have to do something about this sleeping all the time. You're bewitched, she says, she believes in those things . . .'

Sebastián blew up. After screaming at her for a while, he lowered his voice and said: 'What makes me most angry is that you tell me these things as if Mrs. Mechita had said them. Why don't you come out and tell me what you think? I don't want this to happen again, mama. I'm happy to work and support you, because I love you. But I will not allow anybody, not even you, to interfere with my life. It hurts me enough that I can't remember anything at all. No matter how hard I try, my happiness stays hidden behind the door when I wake up. Sometimes I think I ought to drop everything, risk starving to death if necessary, to have time to sleep on and on and on—until the door opens. I'm afraid life is too short. So if I don't have the right to sleep in my time off from work, then it's not worth it to me to go on living.'

'Your life isn't worth living, doing what you do!' Adela answered, and left the room, slamming the door behind her. She locked herself in but wailed very loud so that Sebastián couldn't help hearing her.

Sebastián reflected that trying to explain things to his mother was useless. It was useless to explain anything to anybody. All this was bigger than himself or other people. He was being dragged toward an unknown end with such force that it uprooted him and, isolating him, made it impossible for him to communicate with others. That he could not remember his happiness caused him increasing anguish. Before, when he was a child, he would sleep just for fun, like someone who had found a slightly mysterious toy, but still a toy and therefore harmless. In those days, he slept because he enjoyed it, or when he had time, or simply when he felt like it. But now that he was paying his debt to society by supporting his mother and taking some part in the activities of living beings, he felt he had every right to do his sleeping seriously, in full knowledge of his goal, dragged along by the genuine and increasingly urgent need to know what his dreams contained. What had been a pastime was now his reason for existing, and he dedicated all his leisure time to it, possessed by a driving thirst for sleep, like a person who exposes himself to losing something more important than life itself if he does not make good use of every hour. But when he woke up, the door remained sealed, leaving him bedazzled and drained, desperate to remember the thing that would explain every thing, and at the same time remain in contact with people.

From so much caviling and ruminating on her bad luck in life and the meager satisfaction that her son's incomprehensible destiny had given her, Adela was growing pale and thin, sad and lonely in the depths of her boarding-house room. It finally dawned on her that she meant nothing to Sebastián, she was just another object owed vague affection in the kingdom of objects. It was as if by ignoring her he had erased her from life, depriving her of shape and weight. Adela was deaf and nearly blind, and her legs pained her greatly when she walked. She coughed all the time. One day she coughed too much, and because she didn't have the strength to call for help, she died, as though she had finally convinced herself of her own lack of existence.

Coming back from the funeral, Sebastián removed his hat and gloves, dropping them on the marble-topped dressing table. He closed the shutters, asked Mrs. Mechita to send him food twice a day, and lay down to sleep, eagerly, as if his mother's death had untied the last bond that fastened him to the world. He slept for three days and three nights, the time off for mourning Marambio had given him with a sympathetic look. When he woke up he knew the door was still closed, still hiding the light. But there was a marvelous difference: now he was absolutely certain that one day, even if far in the future, he would be able to remember that whole part of his life hidden behind the dream door. All he needed was to set about it, nothing more. This new faith made him get dressed, comb his hair, and leave for the office, feeling more lighthearted than ever before, strong and sure of himself. He had the secretary tell Marambio he wanted to see him. Marambio received him with a brotherly hug and offered him the most comfortable chair in the office.

Sebastián refused the cigarette Aquiles offered him and said: 'I've come to hand in my resignation.'

Aquiles Marambio leaped to his feet. He could not understand this sudden decision. Why? What for? How would he support himself? Didn't he realize that if he stayed in the organization he had a great future? How could he be so irresponsible? But Sebastián was firm in his resolve. He couldn't see or hear Aquiles.

At last, tired of arguing with himself, Marambio looked at Sebastián and asked insultingly: 'And what do you plan to do with your life? Sleep all the time?'

'Yes.'

'But why?'

Marambio was trying to control his temper.

'I don't know, I have to, I must find out—'

Marambio lost control and began to yell. 'Don't give me that crap about your visions. The truth is, you're a lazy slob, like the rest of you who think you're so special! What gives you the right to a privileged life? Now don't hand me that crap. What you want is to have a good time, doing no work, just sleeping and relaxing. Visions my ass! I warn you, you're going to die and you'll never see a goddamn thing. Okay, get out. Oh, one more thing—just so you remember—don't come to me begging for help. Our friendship is over right now. I'm no friend of professional bums. If you want to take it easy and have a good time, you'll have to take the consequences all the way.'

Sebastián was hurt, but gazed at him serenely. 'What about our bet?' he asked.

Aquiles laughed contemptuously. 'So you have the nerve to keep up the joke, even now? Okay, that bet stands, and it's the only thing between us. But you don't know what a kick I'm going to have watching them dump you in a pauper's grave.'

Out on the street, Sebastián breathed deeply. Now, at last, he was his own master; no strings bound him to anybody or anything, and each second would bring him closer and closer to opening the door. What difference did it make that people considered him useless? What was he but a poor clerk who worked for an import company and lived in a boarding house that smelled of moth-eaten curtains? The dream, on the other hand, although he couldn't remember it yet, would give him a whole rainbow of clarity with which he, Sebastián Rengifo, would be able to drive the edge of darkness back. Yes, now he was sure. What he had given a few spare moments to before would be the vocation of his entire life. He would live in such a way as to sleep as many hours as possible, and would not permit any obligations of 'real' life to interfere. He no longer had any reason to care about things that to him had never been more than shadows: food, clothing, entertainment, people. This way, living near the door constantly, he would be ready, whenever the light shone through.

The only way to achieve this was to strip himself of everything. And, since he had never liked the city, especially now with the approach of spring, he sold his furniture and got rid of all his belongings. He said goodbye forever to Mrs.

Mechita, and she, choking on her tears, exclaimed: 'Son, you are crazy, you are crazy!'

Then he left the city by a road that led north.

The landscape took him in immediately, easing his vigil with a dreamy breeze. The willows rocked their manes beside slow, dark streams, and the same wind that tangled their sad locks gave a different vocabulary to each plant, branch, leaf. Over there, a hill blue with tender eucalyptus trees. The paths of rich brown earth, where poor children played with innumerable dogs, carried him toward an inn that announced itself from afar with delicious aromas, or toward a plume of smoke that waved to him from the roof of a cottage half-hidden in the trees. The bark of every tree displayed a map of a different age and function. Sebastián, in the midst of all this, felt that the distance which before had separated 'daily reality' from the other reality, the more real reality, was shrinking. To him all this rich external world was becoming one with the hidden reality of his dream.

Sebastián, young and strong and happy as the summer began, went along working a while here and a while there, on the farms and in the fields. One place, he helped wash the sheep and was allowed to sleep on the porch. Then he worked in the sunflower harvest and after that he got a job digging potatoes out of the black soil. Then he went on his way while the thrushes hurtled around like stones, menacing the delicate blue of the sky. The money he earned with three days' work allowed him to do nothing for a week; and he spent the whole time sleeping under the peach trees laden with fruit, or in open fields, or in haystacks. The sun tanned his face and arms. A serene light bathed his eyes. When he occasionally went back to the city, he would see Aquiles Marambio from a distance, and at the sight of Sebastián he would turn away or rapidly cross the street to avoid having to talk to him, raising a gloved finger from afar as if to scold him or remind him.

Little by little something strange was happening to Sebastián: he couldn't control his sleep. Now he couldn't just 'start in sleeping' of his own free will as in the past. Sleep would overpower his will, acquiring an independence that ruled him despotically. Now, suddenly, sleep would take over for no obvious reason, on the side of a road for example, and he would have to curl up right there, among the dirty weeds, to sleep. Uneasy, he sensed that sleep was overflowing its place and flooding his entire life. He would succumb anywhere, by day or by night, in cold or warm weather, under the rain or during working hours, and when he woke up his desperation grew when he realized he still couldn't remember. But as he slept more and more, he felt more and more tormented by knowing he was excluded from his own happiness; and yet he felt more and more confident that he would see the door open wide to receive him. A great nearness was what he remembered on awakening. But nothing more.

One day they gave him a scythe, promising him that if he mowed all the hay in a pasture and stored it in the silo, they would pay him a tidy sum of money—enough, Sebastián thought, to allow him to sleep a whole month without worrying about anything, and a whole month of sleep was a fantastic prospect. His chest bare, his scythe over his shoulder, he waded across the pasture from one end to the other. The tops of the fig trees were liquid and murmured in the breeze that had just picked up, and in their thick blue shadows, on the moss, two ducks were resting like recently washed shirts which the wind had softly let fall. Sebastián heard the herons cry out, and, looking up at the heavy clouds moving swiftly over the fingers of the poplars, he said: 'I'd better hurry. The hay has to be mown and stored fast, because there's going to be a storm tonight.'

He worked all afternoon. The clouds lowered darkly.

Sebastián mowed like a man driven to save himself in a sea of vegetation. When all the hay was mown, he knew he was defeated. He looked up at the sky. The rain was already falling. In a moment sleep would overcome him. And he fell asleep on the newly mown hay, the rain falling on his body and on the crop, the harvested hay that would rot. When he woke up, his bosses, furious that he had let the hay spoil, refused to pay him. Sebastián left, walking for days on end, because the news that he wasn't reliable was spreading from farm to farm.

It became difficult to get work. Everywhere he was given a job, however easy, the same thing happened. He would fall asleep uncontrollably. They would leave him to watch a pot, and the stew would scorch. They would ask him to babysit, and the child would fall out of its cradle. They would send him over for a cartload of hay, and at first he would goad the oxen in the right direction, but soon he would doze off asleep and the cart would go astray. The mark of failure engraved itself on his manner and his voice and his ragged clothes.

'I'm getting old,' he thought.

It would have been easy enough to let himself die, throw himself in front of a truck on the highway, or jump off a bridge. But Sebastián didn't want to die, because he could only go on dreaming if he were alive. He felt he was very near the end, but he was tired. The worst thing was that to keep alive he had to work and nobody wanted to give him a job. People would avoid him as if they were afraid of him or thought he brought bad luck. Desperate, one afternoon he went to a psychiatric clinic to beg them to show him how to control his sleep. He was taken care of by two serious, kind young doctors, dressed like angels in white. They patiently listened to Sebastián's story.

'Yes,' said one of them, 'but this isn't an illness.'

'We can't treat you here,' the other added, a bit sadly.

'But I'm afraid I'll die, doctors,' pleaded Sebastián.

'If you spend the whole day asleep, isn't it the same as being dead?'

'No, no, I'm so near, doctor. The door is just about to open.'

'The door? What door?'

Then the doctors decided that Sebastián was one of those slightly unbalanced people who weren't crazy enough to warrant intensive treatment. There were too many truly ill people, and the clinic had to be reserved for them. But they sensed a kind of defenselessness in Sebastián: he had nowhere to go, and was terrified of dying before the door opened. The doctors felt sorry for him and let him stay in the clinic a few days. But one night, making their rounds together, they came to Sebastián's bed and, seeing his smile, the bliss that lighted his face, decided it was impossible to keep in their clinic anybody who slept so peacefully. They sent him away the next morning.

Sebastián knew the end was near. He no longer had any work to do and wandered through the streets and roads, begging from house to house and from farm to farm. Nothing around him mattered. He lived in a twilight world, peopled by shadows, echoes, and waiting. He let his hair and beard grow long. Weakness invaded him and he would walk along roads, railroad tracks, streets and avenues in the city and when sleep touched him he lay down anywhere. Once a horse sniffed his face thinking he was dead. People ran away from him as though he were a warlock or a pervert or a madman. But he went on sleeping, confident that when the door opened all those people who had run away from him would understand.

Sometimes he went into the city, because it was easier to get food there. At the market he could steal bread or a bit of fried fish. But often they recognized him, and a woman staggering under the weight of her packages would confront him and shout: 'Aren't you ashamed of yourself, you lazy bum? Instead of working, you beg and steal. You are disgusting.

They ought to throw you out of town or put you in jail. You're not so old that you can't work.'

But he couldn't work. Sleep would overcome him at once, as if indignant at any attempt to separate him from its power. Once they caught him stealing and took him to jail. They soon let him go, but the word got out that he was a criminal, and the people who used to smile kindly at his venial sin of laziness now crossed the street when they saw him coming.

Winter arrived, another winter, and this one brought Sebastián the certainty he was going to die. He had no strength left. But he thought if he could live a few weeks longer, if he could find something to eat and a place to stay, he would be able to sleep, to remember at last, and he would tell about it. To die before then would be failure. But Sebastián's hope was strong, the only thing in him that did not waver.

It was very cold. At dawn, under the dead black trees of the park, Sebastián sometimes found birds that had died of the cold. Trying to revive them, he would blow on their gray feathers that, hardened by frost, did not move. In the city he lived under a bridge, and by surrounding himself with flea-ridden mongrels to keep warm and covering himself with old newspapers to keep off the wind, he was able to sleep a great deal, almost all the time. He knew he was on the verge of remembering, that the door was about to open. It was just a question of clinging to life a few days longer, finding a crust of bread, protecting himself against the ice and frost. It was hard. Sometimes he would press his nose against a butcher's window and stand watching the hot red of the disemboweled animals hanging from hooks, and whenever anybody opened the door, the thick, bloody smell soothed his hunger and cold a little.

One day he was struck by an idea.

He would visit Aquiles Marambio, who lived nearby. Perhaps he would take pity on him. Perhaps, forgetting what he had said so many years before, he would give Sebastián food and shelter for a few days, though the last time their paths had crossed Marambio hadn't even recognized him. But perhaps . . .

Sebastián made a cap out of newspapers to protect his head, and slowly moved through the cold afternoon, crossing streets—and shadows of houses and trees and unlighted street lamps—from time to time glancing up at the leaden sky striped with electricity wires, until he reached Marambio's house. The clouds drained the red sunset on to the roofs. Sebastián pressed the doorbell. A maid dressed in black with a white muslin apron opened the door.

'Could I have a word with Aquiles Marambio?' Sebastián said.

'With Don Aquiles?' The maid stressed the 'Don.' 'They're at dinner. Go around to the back door, through the alley. This door is for visitors. Who shall I say is asking for him?'

Pronouncing his name, Sebastián Rengifo, was like opening the door of a bird cage, letting his name fly away forever. He waited beside the back door, in an alley where the trapped wind was howling. Sebastián pulled his triangular paper hat down farther and tied the old rags covering his feet tighter. Without a face now, without a name, he sat in the doorway to wait.

At last the door opened. Aquiles Marambio, who had grown fat over the years, had a white napkin knotted under his double chin.

'Did you wish to speak to me?' he asked.

'Yes . . . Don't you remember me?'

Marambio wiped his glasses with a corner of the napkin. Behind him, in the part of the room revealed by the door, some people were laughing at a table laden with food.

'I can't remember. Hurry up and tell me what you want. It's damn cold and the flu is going around.'

He waited. Then Marambio threatened: 'If you don't tell me what you want, I am going to close the door.'

'You don't recognize me,' Sebastián stammered.

'No, I do not recognize you. How am I supposed to know all the bums in this city? Besides, under that beard and filth . . .'

'I came to ask you to give me food and a place to live for a few days, sir. I'm going to die but I can't before I see the door open . . . please . . .'

A cloud of recognition darkened Marambio's face.

'Until what? What door?'

'. . . the door and I can see . . .'

'No, no, no. Go away. You aren't going to die. You are not too old to find work. You wanted to be what you are. Go away. Good night. I won't have anything to do with you.' And he closed the door.

Sebastián curled up as best he could to sleep in the doorway.

During the night the sky cleared and the stars, barely twinkling, looked down sharply from the fearsome black depth of the sky, which let a hard frost fall on the earth. The next morning, Sunday, the sky was fragile and thin, like an immense blue paper kite. The sun didn't warm up the streets but its clear light revealed all the edges and contours of things.

Don Aquiles Marambio, his wife, and his two little daughters, six and seven years old, went to Mass early. They took communion and walked home slowly down the sunny lanes, greeting acquaintances, stopping at times to stamp their feet and clap their hands to drive the numbness from their fingers. A few steps ahead, María Patricia and María Isabel, almost the same size, wearing identical white fur hats and matching muffs, were proud to let the passersby admire their posture and their elegant clothes.

They entered the alleyway that led to the back door of their house, and suddenly the feathers of steam floating serenely out of the four Marambio mouths were cut off. Aquiles and his wife stopped dead. The girls screamed and ran to their parents' legs for protection. Right there, in their own doorway, a hairy, dirty human shape was curled up, covered by dank newspapers. They carefully moved closer. Marambio poked the shape with his toe.

'He's dead,' he murmured.

The woman leaned over to remove the hat that hid his face. Marambio exclaimed: 'Don't be an idiot. Leave him that way. Why do you want to see his face?'

But the woman had already done it, and the dead man's face, under the beard and filth, was transfixed by such an expression of joy that María Patricia, approaching him without fear, exclaimed: 'Look, Daddy, look how pretty. He seems to be seeing . . .'

'Shut up, don't talk nonsense,' Marambio snapped furiously.

'It looks as if he is watching . . .'

Before María Isabel could say what it looked as if the dead man was watching, Marambio yanked his two daughters away and pushed them into the house. They held hands and obeyed without their usual pouts and sniffles when their father thwarted them, and commented to each other how pretty dead people were, promising they would never again listen to grown-ups, who were so afraid of the dead. Marambio called the police to tell them there was a dead tramp at the back door. And because Don Aquiles was a wealthy man with a sense of civic duty, he said that since the man had died on his doorstep, they weren't to dump the body in a pauper's grave. He would pay for the funeral, not a first-class one of course—that would be absurd—but a decent third-class one, which was probably a luxury the nameless tramp would never have expected.

THE DANE'S PLACE

ONE DAY after work Don Gaspar, the paymaster, said he was thirsty. I didn't put up a fuss because any excuse to break the monotony on a ranch in Magallanes Province is a blessing, even if the excuse itself is monotonous. Don Gaspar and I had a habit of going to the Dane's Place on Saturday and Sunday, but by then our thirst was so routine we didn't even need an excuse to go. On weekends usually thirty or forty horses were tethered to the rail in front of the Place, and inside, in the dim light full of smoke and noise and fights, Doña Concepción and Licha went around replacing dead bottles and gutted candles without a word. But sometimes Don Gaspar would happen to get thirsty on a workday, and that was what made him such an unusual fellow. This time, I wasn't just thirsty, I had to say goodbye—next week I was off for good—and Don Gaspar wanted to congratulate Licha who was going to get married.

It was five o'clock. We mounted up and headed off at a gallop down the trail to the Dane's Place. We would have light to come home by, because in the summer twilight doesn't creep in until around ten. I said to myself, better take a good look, since it was the last time I'd be riding that trail, and I might want to remember it later, in faraway times and places. But there was nothing to look at. We didn't seem to be moving, the landscape was so monotonous, if you can call that smooth nothing of the Chilean pampas a landscape, and no matter how hard our horses galloped we stayed right in the cold and windy middle of it. Only the sky changed. Clouds went by, casting pools of shadows that floated or moved with the wind, while the sun calmly made its way across the immense curve of the sky.

Soon, a dark stain on the horizon. From far away, it

looked like it was falling off the edge of the planet; then it got bigger and told us where we were in time and distance. Finally, when we could see it was the corrugated aluminum shack that was all there was of the Dane's Place, something stirred inside us, contentment, peace, because we knew that there, waiting for us, was warmth and wine and different people from those we worked with all day long. Not to mention two women: the owner, Doña Concepción, fat and smiling, and her daughter Licha, skinny as a shadow.

Since it was a weekday, we didn't find more than half a dozen horses at the rail. We tied ours next to the others, and I studied the reddish tint bordering the horizon on the west—to calculate how much time we could stay at the Place—while I warmed my stiff hands on my filly's nose.

Doña Concepción, happy and surprised, came out to greet us. You could always count on a friendly word from her; she was always in a good mood. That was natural enough, she had her daughter, and she owned her own Place, which probably made her a mint: she charged a fortune for everything, and you could spend years trying to knock off chits you'd run up there. But I think we went there more than anything else just to be near her. She was about the only woman in the area —Licha didn't count—and in spite of her age and her fat, she reminded us of a world of pleasures. She always dressed in black because she was a widow. Her puffy white face would break up into big horselaughs so violent that all that excess of soft flesh took a few minutes to stop shaking around her eyes covered with makeup, her fleshy, pale lips, her tiny nose. She led us to a table by the stove, calling Licha to come over and wait on us. The girl took her own sweet time.

Doña Concepción was crushed to hear I had come to say goodbye.

'I'm going to be so lonely!'

Her hand shook a little as she set the glasses on the table, which was unusual, and I noticed her jet-black hair was messy, not like her at all. I glanced at Don Gaspar, to see if he noticed it too, but the little old fellow averted his eyes as if he was embarrassed. His first drink gurgled as he gulped it down his stringy throat, tanned by wine and wind.

'I'm going to be so lonely!' Doña Concepción repeated softly.

I guessed she meant mostly because of her daughter's marriage. She said Licha was leaving the next day to get hitched in Punta Arenas. Then she stood up and her enormous bulk weaved through the kitchen door.

'Doña Concepción seems a little weird today . . .' I ventured.

Don Gaspar didn't answer. Ordinarily, he had a curious way of drinking. He would sit with his body very stiff on the chair and ball up his heavy, hairy fists on the edge of the table, and would never move them except to fill his glass and bring it to his lips. But today he was slouching in his chair, and his fingers didn't seem capable of deciding where to go. After a while, he mumbled: 'It's just that Licha's leaving, and it's so lonely out here . . .'

The fact is, there weren't very many people in the Place that afternoon. At one table three men were silently playing cards around a candle. At another, a lone man tilted his chair back against the wall, took a little sip, and hummed softly to himself, from time to time staring at the cadaver of flat light in the windows, or apparently listening to the wind, which after dragging itself around the pampa, came whistling to cut itself to shreds on the edges of the shack.

'We ought to congratulate the gringo Darling,' I suggested. 'Look, there he is.'

Don Gaspar glanced over, shrugging when he saw the

long, curved shape of the Scotsman, who was dodging tables to keep up with Licha. When she brought us the bottle we ordered, we could see her eyes were teary. Don Gaspar asked her: 'What's the matter, girl?'

'Nothing . . . a sty in my eye, that's all,' she answered.

She barely had a face. Snub-nosed and pale, everything in her face was tiny: eyes, nose, thin mouth. Her hair was nothing but a few limp strings.

Just as Licha turned away, Don Gaspar took her by the wrist. She froze and glared at him. Then she burst into tears. The gringo Darling limped over and wrapped his arms around her shoulders.

'She told him out of pure jealousy!' the girl exclaimed. 'Just so I wouldn't get married. But I'm getting married anyway! I'll bet even *you* went to bed with the old sow!'

'But Licha, what difference does it make,' said the gringo in his half-Spanish, 'I knew all this before you were born.'

Licha dried her eyes with the corner of her apron and, still sniffling, went to wait on another table, the gringo a few steps behind her.

'It was bound to happen,' the paymaster mumbled.

'But what's all this crying and name-calling? It's not as if they were going to die.'

'It's just that Concepción won't give up without a fight. You get pretty mean when you're about to be left alone.'

'But what's going on? I've never seen Licha like this, not to mention Concepción. They ought to be damn pleased to catch that gringo, especially since he's going to be boss some place or other. I don't get it.'

'Of course you don't get it! I've been here for years and *I* don't get it. How the hell are *you* supposed to get it! For example, I don't get Concepción. And I met her two years after I came here, more than thirty years ago!

'I was a grown man when I came here from Chiloé to try

my luck. I was going to work here a couple of years so I could go back home with my pockets stuffed full of money. But like a lot of other people, I stayed and stayed, and here I am today.

'At first it was damn hard for me to get used to it, learn to take the loneliness and cold, so much work for a few pesos when there wasn't anything to spend them on . . . and still I couldn't put any money together. But the worst thing was that a paymaster doesn't have the right to be friendly on an equal basis with the owner or the boss, or with the shepherds either. I was desperate to get back North, I wanted to be any place except here.

'But one fine Sunday I let myself be dragged over here to have a few drinks and forget my troubles. In those days, the owner was a Dane, a man about my age, who had been all around the world as a sailor. He lived by himself. Like me, he was a great talker and drinker, and talking on and on, and drinking likewise, we became great friends. After that my life changed because I spent all my free time here. Also, I started to run up chits, and I guess one reason I never went back North is that I was never able to pay up.

'You would have laughed at the two of us together, the Dane and me. Like any other fellow from Chiloé, I'm short and dark. Well, you should have seen what a hunk of man he was! Big and blond, standing out there on that bald plain, he had a shadow that stretched on forever. He had superhuman strength—which we got a taste of once and for all when he first got here and smashed some drunk's face in—and a big voice that felt like it was going to bust up this tin shack. Everybody was scared of him, especially when he got mad, which luckily was almost never. Then he would give orders in a strange language nobody understood, and seeing as how nobody understood it, nobody knew what to do, and the gringo would get madder and madder until he finally wound up drawing his revolver. But he was a cheerful Dane and had about as much malice as a baby, and so we all had a healthy respect for him; we loved him too. He served good booze. There was never anything wanting in the Place. And he knew how to make some foreign dishes that would make your mouth water. He was a little tight-fisted, though, and he never went to town, which in those days was a day's trip, the roads were so bad.

'Well, one summer afternoon, when our friendship was about two years old, I thought he was acting a little strange. It was Sunday, to there was a mob in the Place. But he wasn't paying attention to them, he'd paid three boys to do the work he usually did himself. He had combed his hair and put on a collar and tie. He was pacing around from room to room, restless, not doing anything, looking, talking to one person for a moment and another the next. As the afternoon went on he glanced at his pocket watch and suggested we go sit on the rail and have a smoke. All of this was unusual, not to mention how neat and tidy the tiny bedrooms of the Place were; they'd been got up to look like a little hotel. But I didn't bother him with questions. Instead I spoke of other things while the silent gringo kept his alert blue eyes on the plain.

'"Here they come!" he said at last, his face lighting up.

'"Who?" I asked.

'He pointed to a dot on the horizon. As it slowly came nearer, I could tell it was an automobile. I asked who again, but he wouldn't answer until the vehicle pulled up in front of the Place and five women piled out.

'In those days, when the city was so hard to get to, caravans of whores would travel around the ranches, staying at the various places. Most of the women were old and ugly, but to us, starved of a woman for years, they all looked marvelous. We were thirsty and there was the oasis—muddy, but at least it was real water. They would stay two or three days, and they were busy twenty-four hours a day. Then they went back to the city with all our money, but a lot tireder than when they got here.

'At the sound of women's voices, all the shepherds in the Place charged out the door to say hello. The girls didn't bat an eye seeing those thirty or forty unshaven men stinking of wine, ready to rape them on the spot. Four of the girls were the usual fare in this kind of business. But the fifth was a big brunette who was still fresh, with a wide face and nice padded swaying hips. She looked like the treat of the century to us.

'The Dane set them up in the little rooms, and right away locked himself in with the brunette, while the shepherds kept the other four busy. The girls spent twenty minutes to half an hour with a man, and afterwards another one would charge right in after him. All of us wanted a chance at the brunette, but the gringo spent four hours locked in with her. We got impatient and banged on the door, shouting hurry up, that was enough, the gringo son of a bitch. Finally he came out, very serious and spruced up, and locked the door behind him. He announced he was going to keep the brunette to himself. We who'd been waiting our turn with her were furious, but we had to make do with the others.

'The days the girls spent at the Place were crazy. The news spread like wildfire around the region, and more and more men arrived to stand in line. The shepherds argued about the girls, which one was the best, giving statistics and advice to those who hadn't seen them yet. Sometimes we had to drag a man bodily out of one of the girls' rooms. There would be maybe fifty or a hundred shepherds in the Place, all arguing it was their turn, getting drunk, stealing wine, breaking windows and glasses. But a great smiling peace had come over the Dane. Nobody could touch him. A few shouts from him settled things down again, for a while.

'It went on for two days—the Dane wouldn't open the

brunette's door and she wouldn't come out. From time to time he brought her food. If he saw it was calm for a moment, he'd spend an hour locked inside and come out all spruced up to take care of his customers. I don't know when he slept because the hullabaloo went on night and day. There was a smell of woman in the Place. The rest of the men who, like me, refused to leave even though they could lose their jobs, slept wherever they could, whenever they could, under tables, in the kitchen, next to the horses, or right out on the bare ground.

'As the days went on, I got drunker and drunker, until the third night I was really stinko. The rest of them seemed to have forgotten the brunette, but not me. I was crazed with anger at the Dane, but every time I insulted him, he'd smile at me and go on about his business, waiting on customers.

'I convinced one of the shepherds who was as drunk as me that we didn't have to put up with this crap. We went outside, brought a horse around under the brunette's window and in the darkness I managed to shinny up to the window ledge. I smashed the glass with my fists, and let myself fall on top of the bed where the girl was asleep. My friend dropped down beside me. We tipped over the paraffin lamp, and that set the bedcovers and dresses on fire, while the two of us fought like dogs for the girl, who was screaming like a banshee. Outside they were banging and shouting. The Dane unlocked the door right away, and a bunch of shepherds followed him in and filled the room. The only light came from the burning bed, where we were still struggling for the girl. They brought buckets of water to douse the flames and broke the two of us up.

'I was drunk as a skunk and they must have dumped me in a corner somewhere to sleep it off. Next day I was up bright and early. The shepherds had already left, or were getting ready to. The girls were in the automobile. The Dane was all decked out. He packed a bag, locked the Place up, and drove off with the girls.

'He came back the week after with the brunette. They had gotten married in Punta Arenas. Doña Concepción, as we called her from then on, took charge of the Place at her husband's side. At first we made bets as to who would be the first to lay her, but a threat from her to call her husband was enough to cool anybody off.

'I was in love, crazy in love. I harassed her all the time, shamelessly, but it was as if she didn't see me. Every day I picked a fight with the Dane, who had already threatened to throw me out and bring me to court for the money I owed him. One night I came across Concepción alone outside the Place. I sidled over ready to take her by force, right there, but she scared me off.

' "What're you pretending to be a saint for, when you're a whore?" I said.

'She shouted that if I touched her she would scream, and her husband would come and kick me to pieces. Humiliated, I turned my back and headed into the Place. But in the darkness her voice stopped me.

' "Gaspar, don't be like this with me."

'It was the biggest, clearest night I've ever seen. Her eyes, heavy with makeup, glittered in the dark. In that moment, something of the truth about all our lives wormed its way into my mind, and something, I don't know what, shattered inside me.

'I ran inside the Place and shouted, "Hey Dane, Dane, come and have a drink with me, you disgusting gringo!"

'The hug I gave him must have been very funny to watch, him such a giant and me such a shrimp. In any case, I think I understood what it was all about, because I never saw him smile like he did then. I swear to you, never in my whole life did I feel so attached to anybody as I did that night to the Dane.

'Little by little, people in the region started to forget where Concepción had come from. The Place was never more pleasant than it was then. Always clean, always something good to eat, and we always had a tidy bed to sleep in if we got drunk or the snow kept us from going home. The gringo didn't drink as much as before because his wife would say to him, "The smell of a drunk in my room brings back bad memories." And she would threaten not to let him in, so he quit.

'Concepción was a model woman, and she was a real friend to me. Years afterwards, I got married. My wife, who was very sober and Catholic, became great friends with her. I never told her how the Dane's wife came to be here, which she thanks me for to this day, because my wife was educated and from a good family, and her friendship was Concepción's greatest pride. After five years Licha was born, and five years after that the Dane croaked, from I don't know what foul disease.'

We sat for a while without talking. The whole silence of the pampa seemed to have moved into the Place. The three men went on playing cards and the one who had been drinking alone was asleep in his corner. Only Licha came and went among the tables, picking up a bottle, cleaning a spot of mud off the floor, serving up plates of cauliflower soup. Then Doña Concepción came over to us, teetering a little. Don Gaspar helped her to sit down.

'I'm going to be so lonely,' she sighed.

We didn't answer.

'And you're leaving,' she said to me, looking at me with the same heavily made-up bright eyes Don Gaspar had seen that night, 'and Licha's leaving me tomorrow to go to Punta Arenas to marry the gringo Darling.'

'Didn't they tell me she had other boyfriends?' I asked, just to make conversation.

'Oh. All that's over. I don't know what's the matter with the girl; love doesn't interest her. She's an oddball. All she wants to do is get out of here. The gringo's got a job as boss for the Suárez family, on a small ranch near Punta Arenas. They say he's going to have a beautiful house . . .'

She took a sip and asked: 'You both know the gringo Darling, don't you?'

'Not very well,' I answered.

'He's that stringbean who was wandering around here a while ago. He doesn't ever laugh, not even when he's drunk. The only thing he likes to do is go fishing in the marshes. He's been coming here a long time, but he's so old and ugly, how was I supposed to guess he was hustling after my little girl? But those gringos are sly ones, all right. Who knows what they've got on their mind standing there hour after hour by themselves, fishing!'

She took another sip. Don Gaspar moved to stop her hand, but she cut him short.

'I'm not saying it's not a good thing they're getting married,' she went on. 'The gringo's got money, and Licha'll be the wife of a boss, which is what she wants. But you know, Gaspar, that gringo makes me sick to my stomach. Those skinny hands, cold all the time, that gimping around all the time. Well, she makes me sick too. You're going to think I'm stupid, but I'd sooner she'd married that maniac Marín when he was following her around, drunk and quarrelsome as he was. But she was such a ninny, she wouldn't have anything to do with him, and then the bastard went North. I wonder what's become of him. He was the life of the party, that fellow. You remember that voice of his? My God, it was like thunder! It got you right here, in the stomach, like the poor Dane's voice, may he rest in peace . . .'

She went on talking, complaining about her daughter, about the gringo, reminiscing, until her voice started to get fuzzy and her words more and more incoherent. Then she crossed her arms on the tabletop and put her head down and fell asleep.

The gringo Darling came over. Resting his hand gently on Doña Concepción's head, he said very softly, as if he was afraid of waking her up: 'Poor thing, she's tight. I'll call Licha.'

Licha woke her mother up and told the gringo to carry her to her room, that she'd be along in another minute. Wiping up the table, she said, never raising her eyes: 'I'm gonna get married anyway, see, just so she'll have to live by herself, that's why—'

'But the gringo's always known all about it,' Don Gaspar said in a feeble voice.

She raised her angry eyes and fixing them on the old man said: 'What do you know about it! Don't you see things can't be the same anymore?'

It was time to go. We wished Licha all the best, but she didn't seem to be very touched. We mounted up and didn't turn around to wave at the girl, who came to the door behind us.

It was a clear night. The wind gusted, hunting around in the nothingness of the pampas for something to tear into while it swept the starry sky. Soon the shape and the lights of the Dane's Place disappeared. Because of the sharp icy wind, we decided not to gallop. We jogged for long hours in silence, knowing we weren't going to get to the ranch until dawn.

Along the road someplace, I heard Don Gaspar mumble to himself: 'I never saw her drunk before . . .'

CHARLESTON

SOMETIMES I think life would be pretty sad if you didn't have a friend or two to drink a glass of wine and have a good time with every now and then. But life does strange things nobody can explain. Just a little while ago, a few weeks went by when I didn't want to get together with Jaime and Memo, my best friends, and they didn't want to get together with me either, or with each other, for that matter. I don't know why. Some things you can't explain. I was very bitter at the time. I didn't even want to turn on the radio to listen to the South American Soccer Championship, and when my kid brothers let out a yell next door every time a goal was scored, I didn't care one way or the other, just because I wasn't with Memo and Jaime and we couldn't celebrate with a couple of good glasses of red wine.

Thirteen days went by without our laying eyes on each other, nearly two weeks. The odd thing is that we didn't have a fight or an argument, or decide not to get together. We just didn't want to see each other, that's all. And it was spooky, because we live on the same block and we're always running into each other without trying to. But during those days it was as if the earth swallowed us up. Just ringing any one of our doorbells would have been enough to get us together again and wipe out the silence between us. But there's the strangest thing of all: although we wanted to be together—I thought about my friends all the time, even at work—we didn't seek each other out. It was as if we were afraid . . . or disgusted.

Well, as I said, Jaime, Memo, and I are great pals. We've known each other since we were kids because we've always lived on the same block. But I've known lots of people since I was a kid and I'm not friends with them, at least not the way I am with Jaime and Memo. Because I'm convinced that friendship is something more serious, more—how can I put it?—more *spiritual* than stopping in the street to say hello to somebody. For example, I think you need to have the same interests. Like soccer, in our case. I don't know if anybody has considered how great soccer is for making friends—you go to matches with people, you buy magazines with stories about the players, and you have something to talk about for weeks. Sometimes, when I meet a guy who isn't interested in soccer, who doesn't know the players or the teams' standings, well, I wonder if he isn't half dead. It's as if he were a Martian, an oddball who doesn't talk the same language or groove on the same things, and well, if a guy can't get excited about a soccer match, I say he probably can't get it up over a naked girl, either.

Speaking of girls, I'd bet Memo never thinks about anything else, maybe because he has such great luck. He's a good-looking guy, slender, fair-skinned, slicked-down black hair, and a sharp dresser, since his brother's a cutter at a quality tailor's and he can get all his clothes on credit. Also, I think his job has something to do with his success: he's a salesman for Ondina Beauty Products—you know, shampoo, cologne, cold cream, all that crap women use to doll themselves up with. That's what attracts them. He's the one who always drags me and Jaime to those dances, the ones they give at schools and clubs, with different-colored lights hanging in a row and chicks that come with their mother or their aunt or their brother. But Jaime and I can't stand those dances and we go mainly to keep Memo company. Why should we like them? Sure, we can make friends with nice girls—and then what? Nothing. Lots of smoke and no fire. If you're looking for friendship, stick to men, I always say. As for the other thing, Jaime and I prefer to visit the red light district every now and again. It's easier. You arrive, you order a drink, you start talking to a girl, and then you get to the point, no beating around the bush. And afterwards you feel so damn relaxed. When you come right down to it, it's probably cheaper, because to get yourself one of those decent chicks you have to spend a wad, taking them to the movies, having a drink with them in the afternoon, going for a walk on Sunday, going to a dance on Saturday, and before you know it, you're broke. It's not as if any of us is short of cash. We aren't rich—all three of us live with our families and have to contribute to the house—but we can't complain, we all have good, steady jobs. As I said, Memo is a beauty products salesman, and although his sector is the worst, he thinks they're going to promote him to a better one. Jaime works at the Ministry of Public Works and everybody knows jobs like that are the best kind to have because they offer you all sorts of fringe benefits and although the salary is nothing out of this world, there's a future in it. I'm the one who's always short of funds, since I just got my education degree and don't have a full schedule yet at the two schools where I teach. But though I'm always hard up, Jaime and Memo respect me because I have more schooling than they do.

Jaime is the least good-looking of us three and sometimes I think it bothers him more than he lets on. He is short and very dark, with plenty of hair in front and a moustache that he takes care of as if it were the girl of his dreams, even though it isn't very bushy. He looks exactly like his brothers, all nine of them. Since he admires Memo so much, he combs his hair that way and tries to look like him, and with the small wardrobe he has, it's pretty funny to see him stiff as a ramrod, holding his head high with his hand stuck in his pocket. I'm blond, and a little on the heavy side because I've got Yugoslav blood on my mother's side. We're all the same age, twenty-three.

But what really brings us together is our love of wine. Now don't get the idea we're winos or alkies. Alkies drink alone and are unhappy. I don't know if we like to talk just to drink wine, or drink wine just to talk. But ever since we were about fifteen, when our pockets were always empty and we didn't have enough dough even to see a movie from the balcony, we would scrimp and save to buy a bottle and sneak off together somewhere to drink it. Eventually we started going to bars and all those places, always the three of us together.

They can dump on wine as much as they want, but there is just nothing like it. In the first place, it doesn't harm your health, the way hard liquor does. We don't like wine just for the relaxation and happiness you feel—as if you'd won the lottery, or some movie star has fallen in love with you. The reason we like it is—how can I put it?—well, because you plan your whole life around wine. Everything worthwhile in the world, laughter, friendship, women, good food, soccer, is better if you spice it up with red wine. Actually, we talk, Jaime, Memo, and I, about wine, almost more than about women or soccer, about the dumb things you do when you drink and how great it feels. In every drinking bout there's something funny to remember afterwards, and every time you mention it, you burst out laughing, and you can't repeat it too often.

'But weren't they better than those bottles we had at that tavern on the way to—where the hell was it?'

'You mean the time we went to the Dieciocho?'

'No, no, when we went to the Dieciocho it was with a gang of people, in Chinchulín's truck. I mean that summer when just the three of us went. This one here'—meaning Jaime—'started in early, and what with the heat and an empty stomach, the wine went straight to his head and he wanted to nail the tavern-keeper's daughter—'

'I don't remember,' says Jaime, trying to play the fool. 'What was she like?'

'Well, she was young, but she was damn ugly and besides, she had B.O. But you couldn't even remember your own name and you kept begging her to leap into the bushes with you. And then her big brother, a military policeman at the post next door, came home for lunch. We were shitting bricks because he arrived asking for his little sister! So then we sat at the table with this M.P., pouring him glass after glass of wine, trying to cover for you. And when you two came back, your clothes were filthy, covered with grass, but luckily the military policeman brother was already stinko and didn't notice a thing. . . .'

We laughed for a long time remembering it all, and how afterwards we tried to pretend nothing had happened, which didn't work because the tavern-keeper's daughter was pissed off about the roll in the hay.

Later, one of us would recall: 'I never saw Memo look worse than the time we tried to kidnap Lucy from Haydee's. We were dressed pretty spiffy that day, since it was your birthday, Memo, and your aunt gave you a huge jug of Curtiduría *chicha,* and we drank it down in a single sitting. After dinner we went to Haydee's to celebrate, and she didn't want to let us in because the house was full of clients. But we slid like eels through a window, and when Lucy spotted us . . .'

And we would keep it up until we couldn't go on any longer.

So that's how it is with us. Your glasses of red wine on the bar, your hot roast beef sandwich so you don't have to drink on an empty stomach, your good cigarettes, your friends all set to have a good time . . . and you go on talking, talking, and drinking, drinking, and you don't feel the time until it's two, three, or four in the morning.

As I said, I don't know how I could have let these two weeks go by without even having a drink, and how I could stand not getting together with Jaime and Memo. It was as if I was afraid of seeing them, as if the wine might turn to bird shit in my mouth, or as if it would stick in my craw. But the strangest thing was, all those days I kept remembering a guy we saw the last night we went out together, and every time I thought about him, I felt kind of scared, or nauseated, I don't know how to describe it.

Often the three of us get together after dinner to go see a movie. That night, since we had some spare cash, we picked a new movie showing downtown, which had something special about it. Instead of just one star, there were three of the honeys—Lauren Bacall, Marilyn Monroe, and Jane Russell. They were wearing a vine leaf here and a vine leaf there and some rags skimpy enough to rouse the dead, and then they did that crazy dance called the Charleston. Well, the fact is, after the movie, we walked down Alameda toward home, warming up from bar to bar, talking on and on, since we're never at a loss for words. That night we were talking about the movie we had just seen, and we were divvying the stars, one apiece. After a long discussion we finally reached agreement. Memo, who likes to give himself airs and says older women are better because they're more affectionate, well, he picked Lauren Bacall. Because I'm on the blond side, I got Marilyn Monroe, and Jaime, who always prefers quantity to quality, maybe because he's so short, picked Jane Russell. We wound up very pleased with ourselves, because although it took us a while to come to terms, there were no hard feelings, as sometimes happens when we start talking about women.

Memo kept saying: 'Holy shit! What wouldn't I give to have Lauren teach me the Charleston!'

We went into a bar, had a round of red wine, walked out, went a few blocks, and came to another bar, until inch by inch we finally arrived at Avenida España. Although nobody would have guessed we were drunk, I better not say how tight we really were. Let's just say it was one of those gentle, quiet weekday drinking bouts.

Memo, the ass, couldn't get the Charleston out of his head. He kept trying to hum it between what he was saying, but since he has a tin ear, he could sing damn little of it, much less dance it, no matter how hard he tried. Jaime and I were beginning to fall asleep, since it was pretty late, but we let Memo, who was bewitched with the Charleston, drag us into one last bar.

'Afterwards,' he said, opening the bar room door to let us in, 'I'll treat us to a taxi home.' This convinced us, and we marched in.

It was a bar like hundreds of other bars in any neighborhood. Long and narrow, with an expresso coffee machine on a counter to one side, and light and dark beer on tap. About ten tables, chairs painted green with wicker seats coming apart underneath, and a juke-box in the middle of the room.

There were only two or three customers left. We sat down and ordered a round of the house wine. The waiter, who looked like he was going to keel over from his aching feet, passed the order along to the owner. The owner was selling slugs for the juke-box to a fat man, and then brought over three glasses of very dark wine, the kind you know a mile off is going to go down like sandpaper.

The fat man was sitting at a table next to the juke-box. He was one of those ruddy fat men, with a happy face connected to his body by nothing but a roll of fat. He was pretty drunk, and although it was wintertime and we kept our coats on because the place was so cold, he was in a sweat. He'd opened his collar, but he was still panting as if it was a struggle to breathe. I noticed that in spite of the fat blotting out his features, they were very fine, his nose, mouth, and eyebrows were well built, which showed he had been born to be a thin man, but thanks to a good life, heavy eating, drinking, and laughing, he had turned into a ball of fat. In the process, he acquired a smile he couldn't ever get rid of.

All at once, it looked as if the fat man had slumped on the table, but it turned out he was just reaching over to put another slug in the juke-box. He had a pile of them in front of him, and we exchanged smiles, because we like music, especially when it's free. All set to listen, we ordered another round of house wine, which helped combat the cold, even though it was pretty coarse stuff. The fat man served himself a glass, and before the music began, he spilled it all over himself. Then he poured himself another glass, but his hand shook so badly that the glass overflowed. He wiped away the spilled wine with the palm of his hand, rubbed his hands together, and afterwards dried them on his trousers. He had messed himself up but good. The fat man sure was tying one on!

The record dropped, the needle squawked, and the first notes sounded.

'Charleston!' Memo exclaimed instantly, electrified at recognizing the tune. He gave the fat man an admiring look, as if to congratulate him on picking the right song.

All three of us turned to look at him, and we practically choked with surprise. Sitting on his wicker chair, his shiny little eyes fixed on a point that seemed to float in front of his nose, the fat man was rocking his tremendous body from side to side, following the rhythm of the dance, and chanting: 'Dancing the Charles-ton, Charles-ton, Charles-ton . . .'

The fat man was so enthusiastic that we started to keep time, stamping our feet and clapping our hands. The whole place seemed to be in motion. The bottles lined up on racks behind the counter and the newly washed glasses jingled as they vibrated with the fat man's rhythm. He moved like one possessed.

'Charles-ton, Charles-ton, Charles-ton . . .' we sang too.

The tables, chairs, blinking fluorescent light, everything seemed to follow the fat man's crazy seated dance. His face was red as a tomato, and perspiration made his forehead and the nape of his neck glisten.

The music stopped. Taking a handkerchief from his

pocket, he quickly dried his face, as if he had no time to waste. After gulping down another glass of wine, he addressed us in a voice cracking with weariness.

'Do you like the Charleston? That sure is music, isn't it? When I was thin, I used to dance it real well, a kick here, a kick there, one two three, ta, ta, ta, tah, tah, tah . . .'

He bent toward the juke-box, dropped in another slug, and the Charleston came on again. The other customers (there were only two of them) came over to the fat man's table, glass in hand, and kept time by banging one hand on the tabletop. They didn't look too happy about it, but since it was the only thing going on, they had to watch and take part, no matter how cold and drowsy they were. The waiter pulled down the metal curtain at the front door, and he and the owner, who'd left off totaling his receipts, joined the group around the fat man, who was moving faster and faster now, dancing with his hands, his feet, his face, his whole body. In the process he waved to the waiter to replace his empty bottle. The waiter served him a glass and the fat man gulped it down, rocking back and forth and spilling half the wine. What a stench of wine there was!

Memo stood up and moved toward the fat man, saying: 'Say, mister, why don't you teach me the Charleston? I'm dying to learn it.'

Without stopping his uncontrolled rocking, the fat man shook his head no. When the record finished, he dropped another slug in the slot. After gulping down another glass of wine, he said: 'I can't. They won't let me dance because it's bad for my health.'

But when the music came back on—the Charleston again —the fat man, like an addict, couldn't resist the temptation. Overcome by the impulse, he stood up wheezing, his eyes almost shut, as if in a trance. He lassoed Memo by the arm, and Memo went along with it, but after a few steps the fat man let him go and started to dance the Charleston alone between the chairs and tables, which we pushed aside to give him more room. He seemed light as a feather and danced with real grace and style, following all the turns in the rhythm. We were left gaping. It was miraculous, the way those tiny feet crossed, kicked, crossed again, and uncrossed with so much agility; how could they support that enormous mass of moving flesh? All of us, the owner and the waiter included, were clapping to encourage him, as he infected us with his rhythm. Toward the end of the record, he didn't seem to be bothering with the tune or the beat; like a broken instrument that frees itself from all laws, he began to dance in an unbridled, dizzying fashion, shaking and moving as if beserk.

The record ended. At exactly the same moment, the fat man dropped to the floor.

'He's turned into a wineskin!' Jaime exclaimed, but softly, as if he were afraid.

It wasn't funny at all.

In fact, the fat man collapsed exactly like a wineskin. But we realized immediately that he hadn't just passed out among the green legs of the chairs and tables like any old wino. The fat man was sick, sick as a dog. He was moaning loud and tossing around. Suddenly he vomited a dark fluid, wine or blood, I don't know, because I didn't want to look. After that, he seemed to get weaker, quieter but also deader. They were trying to bring him around as he lay groaning. He complained like a little child, but I realized something had broken inside that huge body, leaving him unconscious, not unconscious like a wino, but like a corpse.

Well. Let's skip the unpleasant details. The ambulance arrived, the doctor shook his head and said nothing, and they took him away. He must have weighed a ton, because the orderlies had quite a time lifting him onto the stretcher and carrying him out of there. I never heard another word about him. I don't know whether he died, but he might have. It was horrible to hear him moaning, stretched out on the bar room floor and rolling around, his fat face contorted with pain.

The bar closed, and we left without a word. I remembered that Memo had promised to treat us to a taxi, and seeing he wasn't going to keep his word made me furious at him for being such a liar. It was damn cold and pretty windy, which made me even madder. I felt like giving him a piece of my mind right then and there and making my own way home, but I didn't, because—I'm ashamed to say it—I was afraid to walk down that street alone, where there wasn't anything but a few starving mutts tipping over garbage cans to get scraps of food. I kept looking over my shoulder because I thought I heard the noise of a straggler streetcar that might get us home faster, but the sound was far off, coming from some distant street. Jaime, the idiot, had the hiccoughs, which made me even more nervous. When we got to our block, we didn't even look at each other to say goodbye. Maybe they were hating me too at that moment.

The memory of the fat man kept dancing in my head all those days I didn't see Jaime and Memo. Walking in front of any bar made me sick, the same with wine, as if wine, all the wine in the world, had the same sickening odor that filled that bar room the night the orderlies, dressed in white like angels, carried the poor fat man away, after he had been so happy. But although I thought about my friends all the time, and missed them and felt dead because I wasn't with them, I didn't want to go looking for them, because it crossed my mind, who knows why, that everything that happened that night was their fault. And all that fear I felt thinking of the fat man—because I really had the willies, I needn't deny it—was going to make me a damn sight more scared if I went out with Jaime and Memo, because together we would start to drink wine again and I didn't want to.

Every evening that went by without our seeing each other seemed to remove me farther and farther from I don't know what danger, but it also removed everything that made life worth living. Eventually, I went out once or twice around eight o'clock to buy a meat pie from the old lady who sets up her grill on the corner. But it was just a ruse to bump into Jaime and Memo. Finally one evening we met, thirteen days after our last outing—I'd kept count of the days. We bought meat pies and ate them standing on the corner and, just as if we had seen each other the day before, we decided to go see a movie that night.

After the movie, none of us wanted to talk. I know what was wrong. It was seeing a movie and not going out afterwards for a glass of wine. It meant that something about our friendship was spoiled. In our silence, like the one that night, the fear separating us could turn into hate, ruining our friendship for good.

On the way home, we went by one bar and nobody said anything. We didn't even look at each other. My hands were all balled up inside my coat pockets, and I felt the same tension in Memo and Jaime. We went on in silence and passed another bar—and nothing, as if it didn't exist. Before our block there is one more bar, the last. I knew if nothing happened to stop us, to force us inside, from that night on the three of us would see each other less and less, until maybe we wouldn't even say hello on the street. Impossible. The bar was only a few steps ahead. I had to stop and force them to go inside.

But when we came to the bar room door, all three of us stopped at the same time. I looked at Jaime and Memo, and realized that they had been thinking the same thing as me. And when the three of us, standing there, burst out laughing at the same time, we knew the danger had passed. Jaime said: 'What say we plunge in, fellows?'

We opened the door and went inside.

'What are you going to have?' I asked, acting drunk.

'Now what do you think!' said Memo, laughing.

I think we did the right thing. We are too young to be so damn careful. Later, when we get old and our blood pressure goes up, like the fat man dancing the Charleston, that will be the time to start taking care of ourselves. Not now.

And we ordered three bottles of red wine, the best and most expensive in the house.

SANTELICES

I

'BECAUSE I'm sure you'll understand, Santelices, if we let all our boarders do that, we'd wind up in the street. Yes, yes, I know what you're going to say and you're absolutely right. How could you imagine we would deny you permission to hang up a few pictures, when you've lived with us for three years and I don't suppose you'll ever leave?'

It was incomprehensible how Don Eusebio could talk so much when the tired muscles of his toothless face seemed unable to produce anything other than feeble gurgles and pouts. Santelices mused that if he let Bertita tempt him to remove his dental plate—'Make yourself at home, Santelices, feel free,' she'd say, or, 'Get comfortable, there aren't any pretty girls to impress here'—his own mouth would look like Don Eusebio's in no time at all.

'But twenty-five pictures is too much.'

'Twenty-three,' Santelices corrected, stuttering a little.

'Twenty-five, twenty-three, it's all the same. Put yourself in my shoes. Do you know what the wallpaper in this house would be like if everybody decided to nail up twenty-five little pictures in their room? Do you realize? Afterwards nobody would want to rent the rooms. You know how people fuss about little things, always making demands, when I'll bet before they came here they didn't even know what a flush toilet was—'

'Yes, but they weren't even nails—'

'Nails, tacks, what's the difference. Look at this wall. And this one. I don't even want to think about the row Bertita's going to make when she sees this. And how much is it going to cost to repaper the room? You figure it out. A fortune. What with the way those chiseling paperhangers charge these days—'

'But the wallpaper was already a mess, anyway.'

'Just tell me one thing, Santelices. What got into you, suddenly wanting to hang all those disgusting pictures on the wall? And where the hell did you get so many of them? Frankly, I have to tell you I think it's a little odd . . . in fact, pretty damn crazy. Not at all what I expected from you, Santelices. Only the other day Bertita and I were saying that if all our boarders were like you, so quiet and neat, this would be a nice business, instead of the hell it is.'

'That's very kind of you, but—'

'You don't have to thank me. I'm not saying anything but God's own truth. You're more than a boarder, you're a relative, almost a member of the family, you might say, especially because you're such a regular fellow, the way you treat people, you're like us—you don't have pretensions. And I want to tell you something else in confidence, man to man. Don't go round repeating it to people, mind you . . .Look here, well, Bertita, you know . . .'

'Now really, Don Eusebio . . .'

The old man lowered his voice. 'If those pictures were of women in bathing suits, or the kind with a tiny bit of black lace underwear that comes on those pretty calendars they make nowadays, you know, I'd understand. I may be old, but you know me and you know I'm young in mind, happy-go-lucky and all that. And I wouldn't say anything to Bertita. But *this* . . . It's just damn peculiar, Santelices. You can't tell me it isn't.'

'I don't know, but—'

'And look what it did to the wallpaper. Look at this hole—'

'But Don Eusebio, I'm not going to move . . .'

'—and this one. The dirt from the wall's falling on the sheets, which I myself changed for you last week. Look at this, for God's sake. Before my poor daughter sees it and has a heart attack, I'm going to call a paperhanger for an estimate, and whatever it costs, you're going to have to foot the bill. . . .'

And Don Eusebio left the room, taking a fistful of prints as proof of his boarder's perversity.

2

SANTELICES was late to the office.

Generally he put on his socks, garters, undershirt, and shorts sitting on the bed. When it was very cold in the morning, he got almost completely dressed under the blankets in the warmth accumulated overnight. In two minutes it would be eight-thirty, when he had to be at work. Sitting on the edge of the small bed shivering, he didn't know what to do. The illustrations and photos nailed to the wall the night before, which he hurriedly tore down during Don Eusebio's tirade, were ragged, wrinkled, and all mixed up with his pajama pants on top of the sheets, which were still sour with the odor of his body.

Going up to his room the night before, after the canasta game, he knew he was about to do it. The feeling he was going to do it had been building up in him for some time, because passing a hardware store last week he had bought a pound of tacks without knowing why. It was too difficult to go to sleep feeling that those long yellow eyes, those padded feet, those bodies sleek in the warm lethargy of other climates, were prisoners, laid out flat in the bottom drawer of his bureau. It was as if he heard them howling in there, and he couldn't resist, even though it was nearly three in the morning.

Last night, as though Bertita had guessed he meant to do something that would exclude her after going up to his room, she had dragged out the canasta game round after round to an incredible hour. Santelices was sleepy and protested he had to go to work early the next day. But he was less sleepy than anxious to get upstairs to his room, as he had on other nights when Bertita had been less intractable about the hour, to open his albums of clippings and photographs, his books, portfolios of prints, envelopes full of illustrations, drawings, data, articles. Bertita knew their habitual canasta game after dinner, with her, Don Eusebio, and a dummy, was a passion with Santelices, and he would never give up the game while there were still cards on the table. It was easy to keep him there to prolong the match. They didn't play for money. Each of them had a bag of beans—big white beans that looked like porcelain—to use in place of money. On Saturday they counted up the beans. Whoever was losing took the other two to whichever movie they chose. Bertita kept the bean bags in her room.

At the end of the evening, Santelices had been about to fall asleep. The cards weighed in his hands and his eyelids were heavy, until finally in the high-ceilinged dining room lit by a single bulb, all he could see was a salad of spades, clubs, and hearts. Each round, Bertita would elbow him in the ribs to rouse him out of his stupor.

'Come on, Santelices,' she'd say. 'It's your turn. Canasta is meant to be played quickly, especially when there's a dummy.'

'Tonight it seems we've got two dummies,' Don Eusebio put in, letting out a loud guffaw that shook Santelices' dental plate like a pink fish in the glass on the unsteady table.

'That's enough, papa,' Bertita snapped. 'You act as if you were eight years old, instead of eighty. Stop laughing.'

Toward the end, Santelices revived a little, because Don Eusebio began to invent rules in his own favor. At first Santelices, too drowsy to argue, let them pass and he hoped it would all be over soon. But when Don Eusebio shamelessly asserted that you could claim the discard pile with a card and a joker before going down, provided the card was an ace, indignation shocked Santelices into action.

'That's not so!' he shouted, grabbing the old man's hand on its way to the pile.

Bertita choked on the grenadine she was sipping. 'Are you insinuating that my father cheats?'

'You can't, it's not allowed, it's not allowed!' Santelices yelled. 'When I summered at the springs at Panimávida, I knew a lady who had been in Uruguay—'

'When did you ever summer at any damn springs!' the old man shouted, his hand still trapped by Santelices'.

'Let my father go, and kindly control your imagination,' Bertita said to Santelices. 'You know, nothing bothers me more than untruthful people—'

'And he says *I'm* a liar,' Don Eusebio protested. 'Give me a swig of your grenadine, child. This argument gives me a craving for something sweet.'

'No, I don't have much left.'

'You'll get bloated. Half a bottle in one night is too much.'

'You can't take the pile,' Santelices insisted. 'You cannot, you cannot; you're not going to make an ass out of me.'

'Who wants to make an ass out of you, for a few lousy beans?' said Don Eusebio.

'What about the movies? I've been treating now for four weeks—'

'Pooh, the movies . . .'

'This game of canasta is a crashing bore,' Bertita said. 'I don't know when I've been so bored. Well, let's quit, I'm sleepy. The majority rules. What do you say, Santelices? Can you or can you not take the pile with an ace and a joker before going down?'

'You cannot.'

' "You cannot" has one vote. I vote that you can. One vote in favor and one against. What about you, papa: can you or can't you?'

'You can't,' said the old man, distracted because he was staring covetously at Bertita's bottle of grenadine.

Bertita, indignant at her father's muddleheadedness,

which according to her made her look ridiculous, scrambled all the cards together on the table with one swoop of her hand, and stood up. She went off to her bedroom without saying good night, and left the two men to sort out the cards and put them away. But she didn't forget to take along the bean bags.

Going upstairs to his room, Santelices was thinking that he would only have four hours of sleep before he had to get up and go to the office. Through a broken pane in the skylight a drip fell insistently into a pail. From the rooms along the dark corridor emerged the snores of the boarders with whom Don Eusebio and Bertita didn't socialize; they only bestowed the privilege of their intimacy on him. The precise, icy shape of the key in his hand and the minute metallic noise of putting it in the lock woke him up a little. He put his pajamas on. Keychain in hand, he went to the bureau and opened the bottom drawer.

Merely to empty the envelopes on his bed and to spread out some of the portfolios was enough to transform his room. New odors, powerful and animal, overcame the tired everyday ones. Sturdy branches were created, ready to quiver after the ferocious leap. In the deepest part of the vegetation, the thickets crackled under the weight of stealthy paws and the grass stirred with the slyness of marauding bodies. Animal effusions sullied the air. The green and purple shadows and the spotted light shuddered at the dangerous presence of beauty, at the threat contained in grace and strength.

Santelices smiled. This was something Bertita was incapable of understanding. Now, neither time nor sleep nor the office mattered: time had extended its limits in a gesture of generosity. Santelices took out everything. He spread them all out on his bed, on the floor, the table, the bureau, and the night table, and, contemplating them in leisure and contentment, looked for his pound of tacks. His collection was the biggest and most beautiful in the world. Although he had never shown it or spoken of it to anyone, all he needed was this intimate contemplation to feel superior, solid, and proud in the face of others, who would never suspect what he had hidden in the bottom drawer of his bureau.

With his first salary check as an archivist, many years ago, he treated himself to a box of chocolates adorned with a sky-blue ribbon, on the lid of which was a cute kitten of a domesticated species playing with a ball of yarn. After he had eaten all the chocolates, he had resisted throwing the box away because he thought it was very pretty, and so he kept it. He kept it for many years. At times he would remember that smile that was not a smile, that hint of danger in the playful paw with barely protracted claws. Then he would take out the box to look at it. As time went on, he took it out more and more often, until at last he felt it wasn't enough, that the essence of what had driven him to keep it was diluted, almost completely absent. One afternoon while leafing through back issues of magazines in a used bookstore, he came across an article with color photographs that showed not the domesticated species, but others that were marvelously different: the kind that live in the jungle and kill. He remembered his candy box; falling in love with the new things he saw, he forgot it. Here, contemplating the sensational photos, he felt the nape of his neck grow cold with emotion; the nearness of the threat, the naked cruelty seemed to enhance their beauty, give it overwhelming effectiveness, make it boil, flame, blind, until his hands were damp and his eyelids flickered. He paid for the magazine eagerly. After that he began to make the rounds of the bookstores regularly, looking for something to prolong that emotion, to expand it, multiply it, and he bought everything he could find. Sometimes he was tempted by enormously expensive volumes that left him broke for months. More than once he sent abroad for monographs in unintelligible languages, which he would leaf through, caressing them, and it seemed to him he was acquiring something additional.

Sometimes he would wander through the bookstores for months without finding anything. In the half-light of his room, with only the blue bulb of his night light lit, he would pore over the prints, searching for that emotion lost among the illustrations, which remained perversely inanimate, reduced to paper and printer's ink. Something in himself also remained inanimate. The eagerness of his search crippled his imagination, because the anxiety of obtaining that unknown grew like a blinding, paralyzing vine which left no room for anything but itself.

One of those afternoons, Bertita said to him: 'Say, Santelices, what's eating you, wandering around all pale like that?'

It was as if she had yanked away the few things he had left.

At the office one day, he feigned illness and went to the zoo. He spent quite a while near the wild beasts' cages. The flies buzzed around their mouths and piles of fetid excrement. Their tails were dirty, their coats worn and dull, their cages disappointingly small. When the keepers threw them shreds of beef on long pitchforks, the beasts fell upon the bloody scraps, making the bones crunch, growling, spewing off hot saliva as they ate. Santelices fled. This was what he wanted, but not this way. After his visit to the zoo, he was no longer satisfied in his trips to the bookstores by beautiful prints in which the beasts sported triangular smiles and sinuous struts; they did not really hint at death. He longed for ferocious scenes in which the steaming maws would still be tinged with hot blood, or in which the weight of the animal fell in all its brutality on a terrified victim. Santelices' heart pounded with the victim's, and to save himself from panic he fixed his eyes on the aggressor.

Last night he had set free the most beautiful, the princes, his favorites. He tacked them to the headboard of his bed, next to the night table and the mirrored wardrobe, and for a long time lay stretched out on the bed with the veiled light, feeling them rather than watching them take over his room. Dangerous sounds were freed, perhaps nothing more than a paw in a puddle, a twig breaking, or the sudden perking of pointed ears. There were compact bodies with perfect strides, winking eyes that glowed like coals in the dark, mouthfuls of air consumed by powerful lungs, presences brushing by, the heat of coats stretched over elegant, precise muscles: an enervating incitement to take part in an incandescent life, to risk himself by becoming maw and blood, victim and aggressor.

But Santelices fell asleep.

It was less than an hour later when Don Eusebio pounded on his door, and came in without waiting. Switching on the light, he explained he had come to ask a favor—which doubtless Santelices would agree to, given the intimacy they shared only with him: would he please get up early today, because the water heater in one of the bathrooms was out of order and it would be a good idea to put as little strain as possible on the other at the hour when most of the boarders went to work . . . But he never finished his explanation, because suddenly his eyes focused, his toothless mouth fell open, and a second after his astonishment subsided, he began his tirade, ordering Santelices to tear that junk down off the wall immediately.

When the old man went out, Santelices took forever dressing. It didn't matter whether he was late to the office: after all, in sixteen years of work he had never once been late. Going downstairs on tiptoe, his stomach turned at the certainty that Bertita would hear him go out. He returned to his room and changed his shoes, putting on a pair with rubber soles, and went down again, more quietly than before. There was no light on in her room . . . or was there? He slipped past her door as softly as he could, but heard the expected shout: 'Santelices!'

He froze, his hat held high over his head. 'Did you say something, Bertita?'

'Don't play the fool with me, you hear. Come inside.'

Santelices wavered with his hand on the doorknob before going in, examining two dead flies that had dried out over the years between the dusty lace curtain and the pane of glass. Bertita was still in bed, sitting up in the midst of what looked like a sea of fat pillows. On her night table there was an overturned box of powder, a comb with tangled hair, rollers, hair clips, bobby pins. Next to the bed, keeping guard over her, was Don Eusebio, a broom in his hand and a rag tied around his head.

'So you think there's nothing to do, eh, while you keep on standing there like an idiot?' Bertita screamed at him, and the old man fled to substitute for the maid they had fired the week before.

When they were alone, Bertita lowered her eyes and began to sniffle. Her hands trembled on the light blue blanket. Her chest was like a great bubble that kept inflating. The tears coursed down her ample, recently powdered cheeks; seeing this, Santelices understood that Bertita had made herself up especially for him, and he wanted to leave the room.

'Santelices!' he heard again.

Bertita had him trapped with her eyes, which were now dry.

'The thing is—'

'Would you mind telling me—'

'But I didn't—'

'Would you mind telling me how, after all I have done for you . . .' and she began to cry again, continuing: 'All those dirty pictures . . . you hate me.'

'How can you say—'

'Yes, yes, you hate me. And I've been like a mother to you, remember when you had your operation, I made special dishes for you, I stayed with you all the time so you wouldn't get bored, remember I gave you this room, my own room and my own bed, so you'd be more comfortable and get well. You are absolutely the most ungrateful . . .'

With a shudder, Santelices remembered his convalescence in Bertita's bedroom, after his ulcer operation. He had looked forward to that month of rest in bed with full pay and a substitute in the office as paradise itself. All that peace and quiet to examine his albums of clippings and photographs! He could read all about habits, the geographical distribution of the species, their strange habitats! But against his will, when he was still too weak to protest, Bertita had installed him on the ground floor in her own bedroom to have him close at hand, and she spent entire days beside him, suffocating him with her attentions, never leaving him alone for a minute, entertaining him, watching him, seeing in his least movement a nonexistent wish, a meaning he hadn't meant, a request for something he didn't need. Up there, in his own bedroom, the eyes shone blind and the perfect bodies lay flat in his bureau drawer all month long, waiting for him. Bertita had not allowed Santelices to return to his room until she was completely satisfied that he had fully recovered.

'But I think the world of you, Bertita—'

'Oh you do, do you,' she said, suddenly ceasing to cry and shaking the prints Don Eusebio had brought her. 'You do, do you. And you think that gives you the right to mess up my house any way you feel like? And those disgusting pictures . . . That's why you lock yourself in, isn't it, and now I've found you out and now you're not going to be able to do any of your queer things without my knowing. This kind of thing can't happen in this house. We may be poor, but we're decent. You want to have your cake and eat it too, yes, that's what you want, just like all men, you want a girl to sacrifice herself for you and then you do queer things and never even tell a girl . . . and afterwards you hate her—'

'How can you say that; Bertita, I like you very much—'

'Now don't you come and make fun of me just because I'm a poor lonely old maid who has to take care of a useless father who can't even defend her. You know him now, when he's an old man, when he hasn't much longer to live, but you should have seen him before; my God, how he made us suffer! Totally thoughtless, like all men, you in particular: selfish, conceited, a pig, because those pictures, look at them, now don't you contradict me, they are pure filth. And after playing canasta with me like a little saint, you wolf in sheep's clothing—oh, yes. You think I'm a little slow, don't you. Well, I am going to have your entire room replastered, and papered with the most expensive wallpaper there is, and even if it costs a million you are going to have to pay for it. I'm going straight up there to see the mess you left, and I'll probably catch a cold just because of you.'

Seeing Bertita's vast body rising in a single bound from the sheets and pillows, lewdly dressed in a semi-transparent nightgown she had bought from a lady in the boarding house who brought them back after little trips, Santelices opened the door and fled. The smell of the unaired room, powder, sticky pink grenadine, and the flabby body of an old maid, pursued him in his four-block run to the office. He raced up the five flights because the elevator was out of order, went in without saying good morning to anybody, and locked himself in his office, ordering that on no account was he to be disturbed; no one was to ask him for anything until Monday, because today he was checking things. He paced back and forth between the shelves full of papers. On his windowsill, a few pigeons were pecking at something, and from time to time they would look in at him. He sat down at his desk and stood up again. From the window he looked down into the narrow patio bisected by the slanting rays of light, the clouds dragging themselves across the clear morning sky, and at the blonde girl playing down in the patio, five stories below.

He waited all morning, didn't go to lunch, stayed shut in his office all afternoon. He looked out again and again, the sky, the shelves, the girl playing with a cat, trying not to think, putting off the moment when he would have to return to his room to discover that now he had nothing. . . .

3

WHEN Santelices left work that afternoon, he wandered through the streets, heading for the zoo, which was already closed for the night. After circling the iron fences, he stopped abruptly: amid the turbulent multiplicity of odors, he could distinguish ones that were familiar to him. From the enclosure of night cages faint roars reached his ears, growing fainter and fainter. But since he didn't want to see or hear anything, he left when night fell abruptly and wandered on through the streets. He ate a sandwich with a hot sauce that made him fear another ulcer. After that, he went to a movie house that had continuous showings and fell asleep in his seat. When he left it was nearly 1 A.M. Surely nobody would be awake at Bertita's boarding house. Only then did he decide to go back.

In the corridor a smell of burned papers filled his nose, superimposed on the odor of Friday's fried fish—ersatz mackerel—but not strong enough to wipe it out. Silence filled the boarding house, as if nobody had ever lived there. He went into his room and put on his striped flannel pajamas.

For a while, he looked around listlessly for his prints and

clippings, his albums and envelopes, in the bureau drawers, under the bed, on top of the wardrobe. But it chilled him to do this and, after yawning several times with perfect calm, he went to bed. He knew, he had known before he got there, that Bertita had destroyed all of them. She had burned them. All day long at the office, he had been reviewing them in his mind as a kind of farewell. What else could he do? Any kind of protest or attempt to recover them would be impossible. Imagining the prints, he felt like a little boy; Bertita was standing next to him, turning the albums' pages, pointing to the pictures without letting him touch them. Her enforced presence beside the animals' magic flattened the evoked images, drained them of blood, reduced them to the remembrance of the circumstances in which he had bought them, the weight of the books, the varying sizes of glossy photos, the paper, cardboard, printer's ink. The beasts' essence refused to emerge. It was as though Santelices had mentally burned each of the prints in a flame that had afterwards extinguished itself.

He took to rising with the dawn to avoid Bertita and Don Eusebio. At night, he returned very late to fall exhausted on his bed and let a heavy, dreamless sleep overtake him. He lived on sandwiches, peanuts, candy, and his digestion, which had always been fragile, went to pieces. In the office he was the same as ever: punctilious, polite, organized. Nobody noticed any change. Since it was a slow season, he had plenty of time to do nothing, sit beside the window and look at the sky, feed crumbs to the pigeons that visited the windowsill, scan the city's roofs through an open side of the patio, or entertain himself watching the blonde girl at the bottom of the patio, five stories down. She always seemed to be busy doing something: washing clothes, watering a blighted plant, playing with the cat, or slowly combing her hair.

Occasionally he would pass houses with ROOM TO LET signs in the front window. He would stop in to examine the rooms, thinking it might be possible to change boarding houses. He would talk for a while with the landlady, who was invariably enchanted by the obvious respectability of her potential boarder, but Santelices always wound up finding something wrong with it—the light in the bathroom, too many steps, the bedroom ceiling peeling—some pretext to turn it down. But he wasn't fooling himself: he knew it wasn't a pretext. He knew he would never leave Bertita's house. It would be too hard to begin a new relationship with somebody, whoever it might be. The idea pained him, caused him real apprehension. Furthermore, he was old enough to enjoy little comforts and pay a high price for them. Come what may, the knowledge that every night he could play a few rounds of canasta without his false teeth, that there would never be a button missing from his shirts, that his shoes would be clean in the morning, that his digestive irregularities would be respected, as would his tastes, his little manias—this was something so solid that it would be stupid to abandon it.

But still he couldn't bring himself to return to the house at an hour when an encounter would oblige him to take a definite stand about his incinerated prints. It was undeniable that he had ruined the wall. They had a right to reprisals. Every time he remembered it, he felt something hot rooting around in his bowels . . . His prints were burned. But he preferred anything to a confrontation with Bertita—he simply couldn't hold out his hand to her for what was left of him. But the urge to go back, to repossess the canon of his orderly existence, was there. He thought about these things while he numbered documents, or sat next to the window in his office. On the window across the patio, a new sign had been painted: LEIVA BROTHERS. Who were they? Down below, at the bottom of the patio, the girl was sewing. It was a shame he couldn't see her face, which must be especially charming when she played with her female cat; he knew it was female because it had had a litter and now there were five, perhaps six little animals cavorting around the girl, who gave them milk and cuddled them.

Perhaps it was the fascination the birth of the kittens had aroused in him that made him forget his fears. That afternoon he headed home right after work, as if nothing had happened, intending to act so naturally that it would erase all demands on his part and all reproaches on Bertita's. He would imply no disagreeable episode had ever come between them. It would be better to call a truce sooner rather than later, before his digestion went completely to pieces and his feet broke down from so much walking through the streets.

He went into the boarding house whistling. He heard Bertita swiftly turn off the powerful stream of water into her bathtub; she was coming out to intercept him. Santelices skipped up the stairs without glancing at her, and on the landing turned back and looked down, as she stared up in amazement, drying her arms with a towel.

'Oh, it's you, Bertita,' Santelices said. 'Good evening.'

And he climbed the rest of the stairs without listening to what she was telling him.

In his room, he stretched out smiling on his bed. There was something intensely pleasant about this large room, even though it was a bit dark, and this new life without even the dangers of his prints, without the torturing invitation that for years he himself had prolonged day after day, night after night, never really taking part except in distant, harmless echoes. He had dozed off when he heard a soft call at his door.

'Santelices?'

'Bertita? Come right in.'

Santelices heard Bertita's hand abruptly jump away from the doorknob at the sound of his voice.

'No, no thanks. I didn't want to disturb you. You must be so busy . . .'

Santelices didn't answer, to see what would happen. After

a few seconds, Bertita went on: 'I only wanted to tell you that dinner will be ready in about fifteen minutes, so . . .'

There was a tentative pause, which Santelices didn't fill.

'I made that chicken dish you like so much—'

'Which one?'

Bertita's anxious hand lit again upon the doorknob. 'The recipe we saw together in that Argentine magazine, remember? And I tested it on my father's birthday . . .'

'Oh, that's nice, I'll be down in a little while.'

'Wonderful, but don't rush. Remember, in a quarter of an hour . . .'

It seemed to him that Bertita stood in front of the door a minute, no, a second longer than necessary before going back down the hall humming to herself. He waited a moment, wet his face from the pitcher, dumped the water in the flowered basin, straightened his tie, and went downstairs.

The chicken was delicious. He had to admit that Bertita had quite a gift for cooking when she put her mind to it. She seemed to swoon with Santelices' praise.

'You have the hand of an angel, Bertita, the hand of an angel. You'll make some man very happy.' He helped himself to three pieces.

They tuned the radio in on 'Nights in Spain,' a program that Don Eusebio greeted with a suspicious degree of enthusiasm, as if obeying a sign. Bertita gave him a hard look, and when the old man started to tell off-color Andalusian jokes, Bertita interrupted him to propose a game of canasta. They all agreed it was a brilliant idea and brought out the cards. The rounds that night were pleasant, agreeable, quick. Santelices won easily, without a word of protest from Bertita or Don Eusebio.

'Look, feel how full your bag is, Santelices. Isn't that great?'

'Will you keep it for me, please?'

'Of course I'll keep it for you.'

At the end of the week, Santelices' bean bag was ready to burst and the other two were empty. Don Eusebio seemed a little put out at having to take them to the movies that Sunday and didn't say much, disappearing behind the racing page of the newspaper until his daughter yanked it away from him. Santelices chose to see *Volcano of Passion* to please Bertita, who all week long had been talking about how much she wanted to see it, because the same boarder who had sold her the nylon nightgown had told her it was about an adorable woman who seemed evil but was good at heart. They coddled Santelices so much that week that he felt brave enough to ask Don Eusebio to lend him his binoculars, which the old man used to take to the races before Bertita saved him from the vice that had cost them so many tears. Santelices explained it was to amuse himself looking out the window of his office, in this slow season.

The binoculars were, in fact, for looking out the window. Specifically they were for looking at the girl playing in the patio with the kittens all day long.

When he got to the office he went straight to the window, but it was a struggle to focus the binoculars. Anxiety confused his hands and made him think he could always find a sharper focus. Finally he was satisfied. She was about seventeen, with straight blonde hair, delicate; a fatal sign of melancholy in her face seemed to say she didn't belong to anybody or anything. Santelices was moved. Around the girl eight or nine kittens frolicked: tabbies, calicoes, and reds that were the offspring of the enormous cat sleeping on her lap. Santelices jumped when he saw how big the mother cat was. He examined the patio with the binoculars. Wasn't there another much bigger cat crouched in the shade of that trough? And what were those shadows moving around behind those plants? As the afternoon wore on, Santelices saw that from the top of the wall, the windowsills, and the branches of a tree he hadn't noticed before, several more cats dropped into the patio, and the girl patted them with a smile. What went on in this patio at night when all the offices in the building were closed? It's a well-known fact that at night felines become treacherous, something happens to them, they are filled with a fierceness that vanishes during the day. Did the girl live there all the time surrounded by idolent cats?

The pampering he received at the boarding house continued and it was easy for him to forget the surprises the girl had given him. Anyway, and this was his secret, if Bertita's pleasant little attentions toward him ever ended, as he feared they would after each and every one, he would always have this long-distance friendship with the blonde girl who lived in the patio. The security of this knowledge was so great that one night, when he knew they were having chipped beef for dinner, Santelices said: 'I can't stand chipped beef, I want chicken.'

'Chicken twice in one week! Not even if you were a stockbroker! Listen to him, who does he think he is!' Bertita answered.

'Yes, but I feel like chicken.'

Bertita bristled. 'Now look here, Santelices, I don't know what's got into you, always wanting this and that; all because you know we—'

Something uncovered itself in Bertita's eyes, which again, after these months, were dangerously naked. As she rolled up the sleeves of her flowered apron, she didn't blink at all and poured herself an enormous glass of grenadine. Santelices said quickly, before that look extinguished his audacity: 'Say, Bertita, tell me something. You remember those little pictures of mine, some prints I tacked up a while ago in my room and then afterwards I couldn't find them? You don't by any chance know what became of them, do you?'

Bertita almost dropped her glass. Her hard eyes dissolved as she evaded Santelices' glance. 'Oh, for heaven's sake, what a pain you are with your daubs. What makes you bring that up now, when it happened two months ago? Doesn't it make you ashamed to keep worrying about little children's games? And especially after . . . well, after that, I was talking with my father and since it seems that you want to keep the room permanently—'

He defeated her by saying: 'Mmm, maybe . . .'

Bertita's eyes focused on him and remained fixed on him.

'—so we decided it wasn't worth repapering it or charging you anything. Don't worry about it.'

'The two of you have hearts of gold . . .'

He waited for Bertita to let out a sigh of relief and cut it off with: 'But what about my prints?'

'Oh, come on, Santelices, for heaven's sake, stop that foolishness. How should I know what my father did with them? I tell you, I gave them to him. Of course—I don't know how you'll feel about this—but you know I kept one myself, a colored one, thinking you wouldn't mind, and I stuck it in that blue mirror frame the lady in Number Eight left behind when she moved. You want to come into my room to see it? It's just adorable. I'll tell you the name of the animal, nestled in all those great big leaves and those strange flowers. Just imagine, once I saw a movie . . .'

Santelices left without a word.

That afternoon he stayed in the office until everybody had gone. As the night wore on, the lights went out one by one in the front wing, until the cement building acquired a resonance of its own, that of a large empty box. A gust of air, thickly charged, blew in through the open window. There remained only Santelices and the unwary girl among the cats, five stories down. The shadows sank, falling on the tiny patio, lit by the brilliance of green, gold, red, blinking eyes. Even with the binoculars, Santelices could barely make out the shapes the eyes belonged to. There were dozens of animals circling around the girl: she was nothing more than a pale spot in the midst of all those eyes that lit up as they watched her greedily. Santelices was going to shout a warning to her as he leaned out the window; but across the way, the window of Leiva Brothers suddenly lit up and was opened with a squeal, and the insolence of a vulgar laugh cut across the silence of the building. Santelices reached out for his hat in the darkness of his office, then left.

That night he didn't eat at the boarding house. The next day, though, he went straight home from the office, sought out Bertita, told her he had found another place to live, and expected to be moving the following month and she could do what she wanted with the room after that.

'But Santelices, why? What have we done?' she stammered.

'Nothing.'

'But I don't understand.'

'It's just that a lady at the office who's a widow offered me a room in her apartment, because she doesn't have any children and the apartment's very pretty, de luxe, you should see how modern. I'd be her only boarder. Imagine the convenience, and the woman is really very nice. She even plays the guitar . . .'

Bertita, livid, wheezed as if pressure were building up inside her, filling her, until she exploded: 'You men—you always go where the sun shines brightest. Thankless, all of you! Go, if you want, go. What do I care? After the way we've treated you in this house! What do I care? You're a pig, like all men, who are only interested in one thing . . . pig, pig . .'

As she repeated the word she began to whimper, to come apart, crying desperately. A wall had risen inside Santelices and prevented his being touched. He didn't hate her, he didn't wish her ill, he didn't even have plans to move to another boarding house. But he saw that this was what he had wanted to see with his own eyes for a long time: Bertita destroyed, crying inconsolably on his account. Before the waves of his compassion could rise and demolish that wall, he left the room. Outside, nothing mattered to him now, absolutely nothing. He went to bed.

He stretched out on the bed without getting undressed. Somebody was snoring in the next room. Across the hall, a little boy woke up and told his mother he had to go to the bathroom. Some laggards came home on tiptoe, waking up the ancient floorboards. He contemplated the walls where only a short while ago his obedient animals had cavorted, before they had been destroyed by Bertita. Nothing mattered to him, because the jungle was growing inside him now, with its roars and heat, with its effusions of death and life. But something, yes, something mattered, had to matter to him. In the depths of his imagination, as in the depths of a very dark patio, a pale spot grew, terrified in the presence of the menace surrounding it. She thought they were only cats, like the one on top of the chocolate box with a blue ribbon. But no, he had to shout a warning to her to save her from being devoured. He couldn't sleep because he felt the girl's supplication directed at him, at him alone. He tossed and turned in his clothes, unable to exorcise the dangerous animals by his own efforts. He got up, gargled because his mouth was sour, and prepared to go out. He went downstairs without caring whether his footsteps woke up the other boarders. He was in a hurry. As he passed Bertita's door the light went on and he heard: 'Santelices?'

He stood still without answering.

'Santelices! Where in God's name are you going at this hour of the night?'

After a pause, he answered: 'I have to go out.'

As he closed the door, he heard a sob like an animal's cut through the night: *'Papa!'*

Outside, the icy air outlined his shape, separating him in a final way from everything. In spite of the quiet cold, with no wind or humidity, he took off his hat and felt the air caress his neck and bald pate, his forehead and throat, setting him apart, saving him from all concerns except for the girl who was about to be devoured.

He went up the five flights on the run. Without knowing how, he opened door after door, until he came to his own office. In the darkness he approached the window and opened it wide: an enormous window exposing over his head all the darkness of a discolored sky, in which the hot, red moon with imprecise contours like an abscess looked ready to burst over the tops of the gigantic trees. He strangled a cry of horror: the patio was a viscous den of wild beasts, from which all the eyes —yellow, red, gold, green—were watching him. He clapped his hands over his ears so that the tide of roars would not shatter his eardrums. Where was the girl? Where was her smothered shape in that hot vegetation, in that poisoned air? More and more tigers with brightly lit eyes jumped from the wall into the patio. Hungry ocelots and pumas clawed the shreds of darkness between purple leaves. Jaguars destroyed lynxes, panthers climbed the trees which not quite, but almost, reached up to the window where Santelices was scouring the patio for the girl, whom he could no longer see. Everything creaked, roared, vibrated with insects crazed by the danger in the poisonous, turbulent jungle air. From a branch very near by, a jaguar tried to bite Santelices' hand but was only able to get the binoculars. An enraged panther with glowing, faceted eyes roared in his face.

Santelices was not afraid. He felt an urge, an imperative drive, the rediscovery of courage lay in his possible triumph; this was his richest and most ambitious decision, and although it was the most difficult one, it was the only one. The branches down below, in the farthermost depths, parted, and Santelices held his breath. It was she. Yes, she was begging him to save her from this fearsome multitude. Animals whose names he did not know crawled up the quivering branches and birds shook their miraculous plumage in the midst of monstrous ferns. His terrified hands shooed away the hot and humid creatures that crashed against his face. The night was full of shining eyes: up there, in the sky, through the gigantic branches that smothered him, and down below, in the turmoil of wild beasts destroying each other. The thick air of the night, barely lit by an opaque moon—or was it some unknown sun—came charged with howls trapped in its density. There was the girl, waiting for him; she might be crying; he couldn't hear her voice through the thunder of howls, roars, cries; but he had to save her. Santelices climbed up on the windowsill. Yes, there she was, down below. With a cry he scared away an animal on a nearby branch, and, to get down to where she was, he made a fierce leap to reach her.

Charleston & Other Stories has been set by the Kingsport Press in Linotype Granjon, a recutting of an early French sixteenth-century design. Named after the great French printer, designer and punch-cutter, Robert Granjon, the face was designed for the Linotype Corporation by that most felicitous and least appreciated of English printers, George W. Jones, and was first issued in 1924. It remains to this day one of the most enduring and beautiful of the classic faces recut for modern use in the early decades of this century. The display face is Monotype Garamont 248. It has been printed on Monadnock Text Laid Finish and bound by Halliday Lithograph.